HANGMAN'S KNOT

D. B. Newton

Chivers Press • G.K. Hall & Co.
Bath, England Thorndike, Maine USA

This Large Print edition is published by Chivers Press, England and by G.K. Hall & Co., USA.

Published in 1997 in the U.K. by arrangement with the author, c/o Golden West Literary Agency.

Published in 1997 in the U.S. by arrangement with Golden West Literary Agency.

U.K. Hardcover ISBN 0-7451-6953-8 (Chivers Large Print)
U.K. Softcover   ISBN 0-7451-6965-1 (Camden Large Print)
U.S. Softcover   ISBN 0-7838-1976-5 (Nightingale Collection Edition)

The text of this Large Print edition is unabridged.
Other aspects of the book may vary from the original edition.

Set in 16 pt. New Times Roman.

Printed in Great Britain on acid-free paper.

British Library Cataloguing in Publication Data available

Library of Congress Cataloging-in-Publication Data

Newton, D. B. (Dwight Bennett), 1916–
  Hangman's knot / D. B. Newton.
    p. cm.
  ISBN 0–7838–1976–5 (lg. print : sc)
  1. Large type books.   I. Title.
[PS3527.E9178H3   1997]
813′.52—dc20

96–35734

HANGMAN'S KNOT

CHAPTER ONE

The hollow where the Y-Bar riders finally cornered him was lava-rimmed and choked with twisted juniper, a few sand lilies spotting the clumps of bunch grass and bitter brush. At one place a spring bubbled out into a tiny pool lined dark with moss—it was knowing about the spring that allowed the pursuers a chance to set their trap.

Their leader was a man named Jess Croy— the ranch foreman, tough and swarthy, with a face like a fist and hard brown eyes and a swatch of sooty mustache he kept chewed back raggedly on one side. When he saw where the tracks pointed he allowed himself a rare grin, that showed a glint of strong white teeth. He told the others, 'We got him now! He won't be able to drive 'em out of there till they've drunk—more than likely, he means to water his bronc and himself, too. Gives us time to move in.'

So sure was he that he divided his men, sending a couple circling off through the brush above the hollow. Such maneuvers weren't really necessary, there being four of them against a single rider, but the psychological effect of it appealed to Jess Croy. As he said, a man who'd been sure he was in the clear was bound to make a comical sight, on finding

1

himself suddenly, and without warning, surrounded by his enemies.

Croy was just the kind to appreciate that sort of humor.

Everything went perfectly. They came walking their horses through the junipers, closing in from two directions; the shaggy trunks and berry-laden branches shifted before them, and a half-dozen steers that had been grazing there—all wearing the Y-Bar on their flanks—saw them approaching and blundered clumsily out of the way. And there was the spring, with a few tall cottonwoods twinkling their new foliage, and nearby a raw-boned sorrel lazing on trailing reins. The man who had been kneeling to drink, with his hat on the ground beside him, looked up. For a moment he could do no more than blink at the riders, as though he were dull-witted; then, as they pulled rein facing him, he made a convulsive move and stumbled to his feet.

He was not a great deal to look at— unshaven and none too clean, from runover boots to lantern-jawed face, whose protuberant pale eyes darted quickly back and forth as he tried to watch all the horsemen at once. He raised an arm and wiped the inside of the wrist across his mouth, nervously. When the others merely sat looking at him, in the flicker of light and leaf shadow, it was their ominous silence that appeared to drive speech from him—as though he suddenly craved to

hear the warmth of a human voice even if it had to be his own.

'Were you wantin' something from me?'

Jess Croy answered pleasantly enough, 'Why, we just figured we'd relieve you of these here Y-Bars. You don't mind?'

'Mind?' the fellow repeated, and grinned as though it were the funniest joke that had been sprung on him that week. He even managed a laugh of sorts, but it showed effort. 'Ha, ha! You're just kidding. My horse and me, we only happened by for a drink...'

'Rufe Flagg, you are a damn liar! We been following your trail with these steers, for the past hour!' All at once the steel was naked in the foreman's voice, and there was a whisper of metal against leather and then his pistol was out of its holster and its muzzle was slanted at the rustler's head. 'Somebody lift his gun,' Croy ordered sharply. 'Don't take no chances. These Flaggs are slippery as eels!'

Slowly, the prisoner raised his arms; his gaunt face was suddenly without any color. One of the Y-Bar buckaroos, a man named Tom Shecky, swung down from his saddle, dropping the reins to anchor it and pulling his own belt gun as a precaution. But Flagg gave no trouble when he stepped in and slid the rubber-handled Colt from its scarred holster. A second puncher had unshipped a saddle carbine so that there were three weapons covering the prisoner. Flagg eyed this arsenal

3

and wet his lips with a furtive lick of his tongue.

The only Y-Bar man without a weapon in his hand now was Burn Wheelock. He owned a single-action Colt .44, and some cartridges for it, but they were in a pocket of his saddlebags at home in the bunkshack. A tow-headed, average-sized, thoroughly ordinary young fellow, Wheelock was new to the Y-Bar—new to Eastern Oregon and to the intrigues of conflicting interest that, he'd begun to learn, flourished here as virulently as anywhere else; but what he had been seeing and hearing just now gave him altogether a bad feeling. He sat tight with the reins in his fists, as he watched these proceedings uncomfortably.

A ground wind, laden with the scent of dust and pine and spring grass, flapped hatbrims and whipped up the prisoner's unshorn, mouse-colored mop of hair. He squinted one eye against it and said, in a voice that had risen a couple of notes now, 'You ain't seriously claiming I'd lift cattle from a man as tough as Harper Youngdahl?'

No one answered him. Under the silent, probing stares, the prisoner all at once began shaking, so violently that you could see his knees tremble inside his much-tubbed jeans. 'Hell!' he cried hoarsely. 'With all his money, Youngdahl don't even know how it is with little outfits like ours! The winter we just went through pretty near *ruined* us!'

Jess Croy made a sound of angry disgust.

'You know damn well you people have been living off our beef for years—and getting away with it. But this time one of you was careless. You ain't gonna have the chance again ... Now, get on your horse.'

'*No!*'

Rufe Flagg backed frantically away, halting when he brought up against a jagged boulder that had spilled down, at some time or other, from the rim above this hollow. The foreman threw a disgusted glance at Tom Shecky, he who had dismounted to disarm the prisoner. 'Put him in his saddle.'

Shecky had stowed the captured revolver behind his waist belt; now, looking a little uncertain, he came closer to give the man a shove toward his waiting sorrel. Instantly Flagg began to fight, even with those weapons pointed in his face—making whimpering sounds of fright as he lashed out with flailing arms. Shecky hesitated and looked to Croy for orders; the latter, losing patience, booted his animal and crowded it close, where he seized Flagg by a shoulder and flung him around hard, face down across the boulder. He caught the prisoner's neckcloth, jerked it free and shoved it at the Y-Bar man.

'Here! Tie his hands.'

Shecky nodded; he holstered his gun, put a knee into Flagg's back and held him that way while he jerked both arms behind him and lashed his wrists together with the cloth.

Suddenly there was no fight left in the prisoner. His knees sagged under him. He went limp as a half-filled grain sack, so that Owen Davis—the third Y-Bar rider—had to dismount and help Shecky and the foreman get him to his horse and his boot in the stirrup, and boost him into the leather.

By now Flagg was near fainting with terror; his hands tied, he might have been unable to keep his seat if Davis hadn't caught the sorrel's cheekstrap and held it steady.

All during this Burn Wheelock had stayed clear, considerably upset but not knowing what else he could do. He had heard about the Flaggs, in the normal course of bunkhouse gossip: Scrubs, the Y-Bar buckaroos contemptuously labeled them, from old Noah Flagg down through an assortment of sons and cousins and nephews and their slatternly women. They inhabited a clutter of miserable patchwork huts, in a canyon somewhere in the breaks of the John Day, where they bred like rabbits and held strangers at bay with shotguns and old Civil War rifles; they were a nuisance to honest stock growers, because of their high-handed attitude toward other men's beef—and because, collectively at least, they could be mean and dangerous.

But there wasn't anything particularly dangerous about the specimen in front of them at the moment. Wheelock was almost ready to feel sorry for him—if his guilt weren't so

6

obvious, and his crude attempts at lying out of it. It was Tom Shecky who asked the foreman, 'Now what? We going to take him to the sheriff?'

'Clear to The Dalles?' Croy echoed scornfully. 'Better than sixty miles—for the likes of him? Hell! We caught him with the goods. There's only one way to deal with these people—only one thing they understand. Look at his face! *He* knows what's going to happen to him!'

Burn Wheelock could believe it. The prisoner's lank jaw shone with sweat; his eyes rolled wildly and animal sounds of distress broke from him.

The foreman paid no heed. Turning away, Croy tilted his head for a look at the trees growing close around the spring—he seemed mostly interested in one stout cottonwood, that had put out a horizontal branch some dozen feet above the ground. He eyed this thoughtfully, and then he brought his glance down again and by chance it lit on the coil of grass rope hooked over the horn of Burn Wheelock's saddle.

'Well, well,' Jess Croy murmured. 'What's this we got? Looks brand spankin' new.'

It was. Wheelock had bought the rope just a few days ago, in the store at Antelope, and so far he had scarcely used it; now, before he knew what the foreman intended, Croy reached over and lifted it free. Belatedly, Wheelock

7

exclaimed, 'Hey, wait a minute—!'

'We'll break this in for you, kid,' the foreman said, giving him a look that silenced him. 'You can have it back when we're done...'

Having holstered his gun he was already busy with the stiff yellow hemp—shaking it out, forming a loop and then making swift wraps with the short end. His movements were deft and sure, the job he did was a thoroughly professional one; Burn Wheelock couldn't help watching, fascinated. Even the prisoner seemed unable to take his eyes off the work of the tough brown fingers, as the ugly hangman's knot took form. Finally, with a grunt of satisfaction, Croy gave it a final tug to set it. He turned, then, and held up the noose for Rufe Flagg to see.

That galvanized the prisoner. His eyes widened; he cried hoarsely, '*No!* You ain't gonna hang me!'

Ignoring him, Croy signaled his men with a jerk of his head. 'Bring him over here.'

He kneed his horse to the foot of the tree he had selected; Tom Shecky and Owen Davis shared a quick, troubled look, but without comment they closed in on the prisoner. One seized his mount's reins and the other grabbed Flagg's arm, to hold him in the saddle as they worked him into position beneath that jutting tree limb.

Croy, with a couple of experimental swings,

tossed the noose up and over the limb and when he had it set at the height he favored, snubbed the rope's other end about the trunk to anchor it. The dangling noose brushed against Rufe Flagg's face and at that the prisoner let out a hoarse squall and really began to struggle, twisting and bucking as well as he could with his arms pinioned behind him and the grip of the Y-Bar buckaroos holding him. Cries of pure terror issued from his distended throat when Croy, cursing, tried to force the rope down over his head and into place.

It was suddenly more than Burn Wheelock could stand.

Used to respecting authority, it normally would never enter his head to question an order—but he couldn't ignore the animal sounds made by a man struggling for his life. Later he couldn't even remember kicking the roan with the spur; he found himself trying to wedge in between Croy and his victim, as he reached and grabbed the noose away and, in the confusion of their milling horses, met Jess Croy's black stare that was filled with disbelief and quick rage.

The foreman swore at him, in the ripest of bunkhouse obscenity. 'Get out of my way, Wheelock!' he roared.

'No, by God! You can't do this—not with *my rope!*'

Croy's mouth twisted under the lopsided,

9

chewed mustache. His right hand went back and pushed aside the skirt of his denim jacket, and closed about the butt of his holstered gun. He said, 'I'll give you two seconds to do what I tell you!'

Burn Wheelock blinked at the gun; he swallowed an obstruction that had come into his throat, all at once not absolutely sure the man wasn't capable of using it. But he stubbornly held his ground. 'It wasn't your beef he took!' he pointed out. 'They belong to Mr Youngdahl. You ought at least put it up to the boss, whether he wants—'

That was as far as he got; with an impatient grimace, Jess Croy simply whipped out the gun and laid its barrel against the side of the younger man's head.

Cushioned by his hat, the blow was enough to stun him and to knock light and sense out of his skull. His own startled yell ringing in his ears, he felt himself falling, felt the jar of landing limply. There were other yells, and something that could be the thud of a horse's hoofs going into a lunging start. Steel shoes jarred close to where he lay with his face pressed into the dirt.

He didn't know how long he lay there, or if he completely lost consciousness. It could not have been more than minutes. When his senses began to clear, his head rang like a bell but there seemed to be stillness all around him. He heard himself groan as he got his palms under

10

him. A sense of urgency drove him and after some shaky effort he managed to achieve a sitting position.

Every tooth on the left side of his jaw seemed to ache. He groped a hand upward and found that his hat was still in place, but dented by the smash of the gun barrel. And then a movement caught the corner of his eye; he tilted his head and, cut off by the brim of his hat, saw beside him the toes of a pair of worn and scuffed cowhide boots. They dangled, pointing at the ground, turning in a slow circle and then slowly unwinding in the opposite direction. Burn Wheelock stared at the boots, and checked the impulse to lift his head farther; he was engulfed by a sudden sick certainty that he didn't want to see more.

Carefully keeping his eyes averted, he rolled to hands and knees. A horse stomped and rattled its bit chain; he looked that way and saw the two Y-Bar buckaroos, Shecky and Davis, standing by their mounts as though they had not moved at all. Neither spoke. Wheelock returned their stares, and after a moment they both broke gaze and looked at the ground—he thought, like men with guilty consciences.

Jess Croy said, somewhere in back of him, 'Get up! You ain't hurt.'

Wheelock's jaw clamped down on the reply he didn't trust himself to make. In order to look around at the foreman, he would have to see the body of the hanged man and he didn't

11

feel up to that. Instead, not answering he maneuvered himself carefully onto his legs.

A few yards away the spring bubbled into its rock basin. He swayed a little as he stumbled to it, dropped down on his knees and shoved both hands wrist-deep into the clear, icy water. He stayed that way a moment, then proceeded to splash his face, gingerly pushing aside the hat so he could explore the lump that had formed behind his ear. It was painful enough to the touch, but the skin didn't appear broken. Shock of the cold water helped considerably to clear the cotton out of his head. He cupped some in his palms and sucked it up, and shook his hands to dry them.

Kneeling there, he could feel the others watching him in a stretching stillness. All kinds of hot and angry words trembled behind his lips but nothing he could say would make any difference now; he let his silence say it for him. Rubbing both palms across his wet face, he drew his hat into place gingerly, and then pushed up once more to his feet.

His roan stood nearby; the sorrel Rufe Flagg had ridden seemed to have disappeared—Wheelock judged that once it had been swatted out from under the doomed man, and left him swinging on the noose, it must simply have kept going. He went to his own animal and took the reins, paused to gather his strength for the climb into the saddle. 'You leaving us?' Jess Croy spoke with heavy amusement. 'Ain't you

12

gonna wait for your rope?'

Wheelock shuddered. 'You can go to hell!' he cried, in a hoarse, outraged voice. 'All of you!' And he caught the pommel, shoved his boot into the stirrup and swung up. In doing so he inadvertently had a glimpse of that silent shape, its head bent at a grotesque angle, hanging motionless in the dapple of light and tree shadow; he passed it over hastily but not before it was indelibly printed in his mind, as well as the image of Jess Croy seated on his gray and staring at him with mockery in his grin.

The buckaroo's mouth set hard, in revulsion. Then Burn Wheelock had put his back to that group by the spring. He gave the roan the spur.

CHAPTER TWO

He rode up out of the hollow, skirting dark, rough chunks of lava boulder, and met the steady buffeting wind that combed this high Oregon rangeland.

Thin-soiled, almost treeless except in deep canyons carved into its lava shield by swift-moving streams, the rich bunch grass made it prime cattle country. Over east, the land began to break up into eroded palisades and pinnacles of the John Day tributaries; to the

13

south rose the timbered spine of the Ochocos—
and beyond those hills lay the Prineville
country Burn Wheelock hadn't yet seen.
Westward, volcanic peaks of the Cascade
Range marched in silhouette, still capped with
white from last winter's snows. For a man
barely into his twenties, Burn Wheelock had
seen quite a bit of rugged country across the
northern tier of states, and worked cattle in a
lot of it. Some was more spectacular, but this
had a certain rock-ribbed grandeur that he
liked.

Or, until today he had liked it.

Once, looking back, he observed movement
following him—the Y-Bar crewmen had
caught up the half-dozen steers that Flagg had
stolen, and were hazing them again toward
range where they belonged. After his initial
burst of speed Wheelock had eased the roan
into a more comfortable gait, that was less
bothersome for the sore ache in his head; now
he saw that one rider, on a gray horse, had
pulled away leaving the other pair to manage
the cattle. It appeared he had in mind to
overtake Wheelock. The latter's mouth
hardened and at once he gave his horse a
kick—he sure as the devil had nothing he
wanted to say to Jess Croy!

When he looked again some minutes later,
Croy seemed to have got the hint for he had
dropped back and was no longer trying to close
the distance. Wheelock grunted in satisfaction

14

and eased up on the pace; but he stayed wary, and ready to increase it.

* * *

The section of deeded land that held Harper Youngdahl's ranch headquarters was well situated, in a broad stream valley where there was grass, flowing water, and rimrock walls to deflect the worst winter storms. Here Youngdahl had fenced off his holding pastures and erected stout juniper-pole stockpens, as well as log buildings that had a temporary look—as though he intended, sometime or other, to replace them with something more elaborate. There was nothing fancy about the Y-Bar but it had a serviceable look. And the same could have been said about Harper Youngdahl.

He was greasing a wagon axle when Burn Wheelock rode into the yard—a menial sort of job, that almost any rancher but Youngdahl might have relegated to an underling, but the Y-Bar owner wasn't one to think of such things: If he saw a job that needed doing and had nothing else pressing, he put his own hand to it. His sleeves were rolled up; he had the tar bucket and, with the wagonbox jacked and one wheel removed, was working at the task with complete absorption—a solid, impressive figure of a man, ropes of muscle showing on his forearms, and a salting of gray in the heavy black mane and beard and brows that set off the leonine cast of his face.

He looked up as Wheelock approached, and his sharp black stare seemed to read the buckaroo's frowning look. 'Something wrong?'

Yard dust spurted and settled under the bronc's hoofs. Reining down, Burn Wheelock regarded his employer. He said bluntly, 'I'd like to draw any time I got coming, Mr Youngdahl. I'm quitting.'

'Oh?' At this the other man straightened to his feet. In everything he did Youngdahl's movements were deliberate and unhurried—not with the ponderous slowness of some dull-witted and muscle-heavy men, but rather as though a sharp intellect weighed each action in advance and allowed himself only the ones that counted. Now he took a rag hanging on the side of the wagonbox and began to wipe his hands with it. 'You going to tell me why?'

Burn Wheelock pointed with his chin toward Jess Croy, just now riding up past the pens at the foot of the yard. 'Ask *him!*'

Youngdahl followed his glance, then looked at Wheelock again with his shrewd eyes. He seemed to weigh the unexplained tensions that he felt here, and after a moment he nodded. 'All right. Sorry to see you go—but, I never believed in putting pressure on a man.' Tossing aside the rag, he took a wad of greenbacks from a pocket; he did some mental calculation,

16

peeled off bills and, adding a few silver coins, handed them up to the other man, saying, 'I think you'll find that's accurate.'

Wheelock didn't bother to count it. He shoved the money into his jeans, muttered, 'Thanks.' Without a further look at Croy he jerked the horse around and headed off toward the low, shake-roofed structure where the crew had their quarters.

The long room seemed unnaturally quiet and empty—plenty of work, at this season, to keep the entire crew out on the range from dawn to dusk. Wheelock had little enough in the way of possessions and it didn't take much time to strip the blankets from his bunk, assemble his belongings and lash them together in a saddle roll. Afterward he looked around, making sure he hadn't forgotten anything.

A string of bunkhouses were a cowpuncher's home, but he was not apt to grow sentimental about leaving any of them—they were all pretty much alike, with the same smells of dirty clothes and man-sweat and stale tobacco smoke, the same scatter of chips and playing cards on the round deal table, the same *Police Gazette* pictures on the walls. Impersonal as a barracks, in time they melted into a common impression of a place where lonely, single men, drugged with fatigue and monotonous labor, made what they could of their free hours. There were always good fellows that you liked,

17

and one or two you fought with; but after a season you drifted on somewhere else and individual faces became blurred, like the court cards in a shuffled poker deck.

Burn Wheelock shouldered his gear and saddlebags, took his yellow slicker off its nail and carried them all out to his waiting horse.

It was his own horse, a blue roan with a Wyoming brand, that had brought him to this job and would now carry him away again. He lashed his belongings in place behind the cantle, checked his cinch knot. Yonder, he saw that Jess Croy had halted beside his boss and was bending in the saddle, in close conversation with Harper Youngdahl. Wheelock could feel the looks they directed at him, but he deliberately paid no heed. He had swung up and was settling his boots in the stirrups, when he heard his name called.

Youngdahl was walking toward him, and he held where he was, waiting. The rancher placed fists on hips and canted his head sidewise, as his keen stare studied the other. He looked troubled.

'Jess has been telling me what happened. A pretty grim business—I guess I can understand you not wanting to talk about it. You never saw a man hanged before?'

'No,' Wheelock answered coldly.

'I don't imagine I'd enjoy it, either—even if sometimes there isn't any other way. Maybe Jess acted hasty, but he did it for the brand; I

18

back him now that it's over. You understand me?'

Burn Wheelock looked over his head, at the foreman who was walking his horse toward them. Croy was darkly scowling. The buckaroo took a long breath. 'I understand, I guess. But just the same—after this, I don't figure I can ride for this outfit no more.'

'Passing judgment, are you?'

'I'm trying hard not to! I just can't see stringing a man up like a side of meat—for whatever reason!' He might have said: *You weren't there. You didn't hear Rufe Flagg scream and beg for mercy; and afterward you didn't see him dangle with the rope creaking and his boot toes pointed at the ground!* But there was no good in that, so he added—a little lamely, he thought: 'This ain't the old frontier. It's the 1880s. We should be past such ways of doing.'

Jess Croy had halted within listening distance. 'With scum like the Flaggs hanging on,' he retorted, 'to steal a legitimate spread blind? They need the lesson!' A sneer lifted a corner of his heavy mustache. 'What the hell's sticking in your craw? Me borrowing your nice new rope, without asking?'

'That's enough, Jess!' his employer told him sharply. To Burn Wheelock, the rancher continued: 'I respect your point of view, Wheelock. I don't hold it against you, and I won't ask you to change your mind. Anybody wants to know, I'm perfectly glad to tell them you been a hard worker for me, and a good hand on my payroll. Still, these are bad times,' he added. 'Has it occurred to you, another job might not be easy to find, hereabouts?'

'I'm aware of that.' For just an instant, Youngdahl's manner had him wavering— perhaps he was being a damn fool, to take a position and blindly hold to it. But then he looked at Jess Croy, and saw the foreman's scornful stare, and his own anger hardened to resolution. 'I'll make out.'

'Just where do you expect to be riding from here, Wheelock?' the foreman demanded.

Burn Wheelock met his look coldly. 'Even if I knew, I don't see it's any of your business!'

'No?' A forward thrust of Croy's head emphasized the challenge. 'They got a new sheriff at The Dalles—I hear he's pretty tough. You wouldn't be thinking, would you, of heading that way and giving him an earful about all this?'

'What's the matter, Jess?' Burn Wheelock retorted. 'Getting uneasy now that it's done? Seems sort of late, to start worrying about the tough sheriff. From what I hear,' he suggested, not put off by the quick danger in Croy's scowl, 'the Flaggs are pretty tough themselves. They aren't apt to let this go, until they've found out who was behind it.'

'Maybe you intend to tell them?'

Burn Wheelock stared at him, then turned to

the Y-Bar owner. 'Do *you* believe that, Mr Youngdahl?'

The rancher slowly shook his head. 'No. No, I don't,' he said. 'I don't think you're the kind who'd want to bring trouble on an outfit he once rode for.' He gave a stern look to his foreman. 'So let him alone, Jess, since the boy's made up his mind.

'With luck,' he continued, 'there's a chance the whole thing will blow over—after all, it ain't like we're the only ones ever had a quarrel with the Flaggs. Could be this will actually teach them a lesson they been needing, so it won't be necessary for anyone to do it again. At least we can hope!'

He closed the argument by turning and walking away across the dusty yard to the house. Burn Wheelock watched him go. Then, with the reins in his hands, he looked once more at the foreman. 'I'm curious,' he said bluntly. 'After I was gone, did you cut Rufe Flagg down off that tree? Or just leave him hanging?'

Croy's shrug was answer enough. 'Hell! Let the Flaggs cut him down.'

'That don't sound decent. He maybe wasn't much of a man, but he was a human being all the same.'

'I *asked* if you wanted your rope back,' the foreman pointed out.

'Not after what it was used for!' the buckaroo snapped back at him. The dull ache

21

of that swelling on his skull reminded him of a further score with this man, and his mouth hardened. 'Just one more thing, Croy: Being the boss gave you no license to use a gunbutt on me. You better not ever try it again!'

And he booted his roan and left there. He didn't look back.

He was seething, all but trembling with anger. Later, as he began to cool down some, he found himself regretting just a little the tone he'd taken with Harper Youngdahl. After all, Youngdahl was an honorable man, and Flagg's death hadn't been his doing; it was easy enough to be stuffy and righteous, when you didn't have the responsibility of a spread like Y-Bar on your shoulders—or the need to back up an employee who, after all, had for long served well and efficiently as your range boss.

Burn Wheelock even began to wonder if he mightn't have been a damn fool to walk away from a good job, over a mere matter of principle. Right now, if he were to turn around and offer Youngdahl an apology he didn't doubt the man would hire him back, without a word ... But then he remembered Jess Croy, and knew the idea was worthless. His bruised skull began to throb harder at the very thought of it.

Croy might be a passable foreman, but Burn Wheelock knew he could never work under him again. He had to go.

But—go where?

22

He pulled up and eased over more comfortably in the saddle, a knee hooked about the horn, and rolled up a smoke with hands that were steady enough, now. While he worked, he thought about his problem.

The pay he'd collected from Youngdahl wasn't enough to last long. Normally that wouldn't have mattered, it being the time of year when cow outfits did their hiring—trouble was, these were anything but normal times. People he'd met in this Oregon country seemed unable to talk about anything except the winter they'd just been through. They named it the worst on record, a winter when a few ranchers with money enough—or foresight enough, like Harper Youngdahl—to put up feed for their herds had been able to bring them through in some fashion, while all the others who according to custom shoved their stock out onto open range to fend for themselves had suffered terrible losses. They'd only found what was left after the unending sequence of blizzards and ice storms finally dragged to a close, and spring thaw revealed at last the full horror of destruction.

He'd seen the evidence himself. One never knew, riding the silent ridges, when some stream-bed canyon or draw would reveal a pileup of rotting carcasses, where cattle had drifted before the knifing winds and piled up to die. The scavengers were having a field day, on the leavings of that season of white death; to a

23

stockman, it was enough to break his heart.

Squinting against cigarette smoke, Burn Wheelock drew a mental map of this area—spotting the various spreads, totting up what he knew about them. Most were one-man homestead ranches, signing on at best no more than a couple of extra hands for the busy season; these already would be hired up by now, and not worth the bother of asking ... But then he thought of Fred Adler.

They'd met on the street in Antelope, the day he arrived, and Adler had given every indication of liking him—only, he hadn't been in a position to know just when he could hire. Instead, it was he who had touted Wheelock onto trying at Y-Bar. He seemed to know just about everything and everybody, and it occurred to Wheelock his smartest move was to look the old German up. Probably there'd be no quicker way of learning his chances of catching on somewhere, or if he was simply wasting his time looking for work here and ought to try another part of the country.

He unhooked his knee, stubbed his smoke against the horn of his saddle and swung north, knowing the general direction of Adler's spread.

Once, riding the silent hills, he spotted a couple of horsemen some distance to the left of him and reined in a moment—he had a hunch they were Tom Shecky and Owen Davis, who had been involved in the hanging, and who by

24

now would have finished their job of pulling those half-dozen stolen steers back onto Y-Bar grass and turning them out there. He didn't particularly want to talk to that pair, and he reined in by a juniper and stayed quiet and out of sight till he was sure their paths were not going to cross.

He was wishing he could simply forget Rufe Flagg ever existed.

But it wasn't as easy as that. As he rode on toward Adler's, a thought that had been nagging at him, and that he had earlier pushed out of his mind, began working at him again with renewed insistence. It grew all the more bothersome when he discovered the course he was following was going to take him within a short distance of that hollow, and the hanging tree. Sure enough, he topped a lava ridge and there, through the slanting light of afternoon, made out a spot of bright green where aspen and cottonwood crowded about the spring.

Burn Wheelock stared at it for a long time, narrow-eyed; suddenly he slapped a palm against his saddle swell and said aloud, 'No, by God! It *ain't* decent.' Repelled and reluctant, but feeling he had no choice, he shook his head and swung his bridles in that direction. He touched his roan with the spur, not giving himself time to lose his resolution.

His knowing what he would see lent an eeriness to the quiet of the hollow, that was broken only by a slight whisper of wind

25

moving through juniper branches. So quiet was it that the faint burbling of the spring reached him clearly before he came in sight of it. And then, prepared as he was, there was the quick clutch at his throat and he reined in, unable for a moment to do more than stare, in a kind of fascination, at the dangling figure twisting slowly and then as slowly unwinding.

The rope creaked faintly. A fly came bumbling by, to hover briefly with the sunlight on its iridescent wings and then whisk away again. Wheelock discovered a tight cramping across his shoulders; he shrugged to ease it, and walking his horse forward placed a hand on the yellow rope that angled up from the place where it was anchored to the cottonwood trunk. Through it he could feel the stretch and strain of the dead weight it supported. On a sudden resolution he dug his clasp knife out of a pocket of his jeans, thumbed it open, and started to work. The blade was dull and he had to hack at the rope with main strength, a strand or two at a time; when the last one parted, he barely managed to catch the suddenly freed end and eased Rufe Flagg to the ground, standing in his stirrups to do so. Afterward, having pocketed the knife again, he got down from the saddle.

It had seemed grossly wrong to leave the dead man hanging, but now he realized he had no idea what on earth to do with him—it would be every bit as bad to let him lie here for the varmints to get at. He rubbed his jaw in helpless uncertainty.

That damned noose, drawn so tight it seemed hideously imbedded in the hanged man's throat! By all that was decent it should be removed. Gingerly he knelt, trying hard not to look at the horror of the face above it; but when he made a first tentative attempt at loosening the stiff hemp he inadvertently touched the cold flesh, and felt the unnatural way Flagg's head wobbled. It was too much. His face suddenly hot, unable to breathe, Burn Wheelock blundered to his feet. He turned violently away, placed a hand against the tree trunk and leaned there as he swallowed convulsively, fighting down the sickness that rose through his throat and chest.

Metal struck lava rock, a single ringing note. His head wavered up and he stared, almost too miserable to register the warning of horsemen filing toward him through the flicker of light and tree shadow.

CHAPTER THREE

There were five of them, tough-looking men on tough-looking horses. They were all armed, and something in the way they came at him helped to scare the nausea from Burn Wheelock's system. Breathing shallowly, he

27

stood there beside Rufe Flagg's body and ran his glance from one to another as they closed in on him—just so, it occurred to him suddenly, Flagg himself had stood in almost the same spot, earlier, watching the men from Y-Bar move nearer and probably knowing he was doomed.

Wheelock had never seen any of these before but he'd have had no doubt as to who they were, even without the evidence in the form of a saddled horse one of the five was leading, and which he recognized at once as Rufe Flagg's own animal. They were all as alike as hounds from the same litter—the litter that had produced Rufe Flagg: Their faces all seemed to work variations on the same structure of lantern-jawed boniness and pale, slightly protruding eyes above slanted cheekbones.

One seemed to be their leader for he was older than the rest, old enough to have been, plainly, the sire of at least part of them. He wore his gray hair to the shoulders of his denim jacket, and seemed to have a cast in one eye— though the way he kept shifting, to peer at Burn Wheelock first with one eye and then the other, it would have been hard to say exactly which was the damaged one.

Noah Flagg raked Wheelock from head to foot, and looked with bitter interest at the dead man on the ground beneath the trees. 'All right, you!' he ordered, in a crisp nasal voice. 'Stand away from him. And if you're thinking of a gun, you better not.'

'I'm not armed,' Burn Wheelock said. His revolver was still in the saddlebags, strapped on his roan. Seeing the threat in the weapons that he faced, he thought that was just as well—a gun would not have done him any good.

The old fellow jerked his head at one of the others. 'Homer! Check him out.'

One strapping fellow, with a wiry beard that had glints of red in it, stepped down from the saddle and approached Wheelock. The latter stood quite still, making no protest when Homer Flagg jerked aside the tails of his jacket and satisfied himself there was no weapon of any kind on him. 'Looks like he's clean, Pa. Case knife in his pocket, and that's all.'

Burn Wheelock tried to meet the weight of the stares beating at him. The rest all seemed to be waiting on Noah Flagg, and the old man took his time. Gray beard stubble glinted on his hollow cheeks as he waggled his jaw, worrying a nubbin of chewing tobacco while he considered the stranger.

'Appears you got some explaining to do. You're a new one, to me. What outfit you ride for?'

Burn Wheelock tried to swallow the brassy tang of fear. Knowing himself to be an unconvincing liar, he determined to stick as near the truth as possible. 'I'm not riding for anyone, at the moment,' he answered—

29

factually enough. 'I'm sort of looking for work.'

'Strange brand on that horse,' someone observed.

Wheelock explained quickly, 'It's a Wyoming brand—I got a bill of sale.' He added, 'I drift around a lot. Rode up here a minute ago and found this man hanging. Seemed like somebody ought to cut him down.'

'I think he's lying!' one of the men broke in—one who looked a little sharper, a little shrewder, than the rest. 'You ask me, Pa, he knows a hell of a lot more than he wants to say!'

Lank gray hair brushed the old man's shoulders as he nodded—eyes narrowed, jaw working thoughtfully on the nubbin of tobacco. 'All right, Mason,' he said. 'I *didn't* ask you, but you're on record...'

Homer Flagg had been examining the body. He straightened, shaking his head. 'Rufe's getting cold already. He's been dead awhile. Whoever tied this knot, knew what he was doin'—it snapped his neck clean.'

'Did *you* tie it?' Noah Flagg demanded of the prisoner.

'Hell, no!' Wheelock exclaimed, in indignation. 'I don't know about such things.'

'It seems mighty strange. We find my boy's saddled horse running loose, and we backtrack and find you standing over his poor carcass.

30

What's your name, mister?'

Burn Wheelock told him, and held his breath when it occurred to him—too late—there was a chance they might have heard of someone of such name working for Y-Bar, however briefly; but it brought no flicker of recognition in any of the faces that confronted him. For a moment no one spoke, while all those pale eyes studied him, and warm wind rocked the tree branches and the spring burbled over its mossy stones. The horses, growing restless, began to move around a little.

'You still claim, then,' Noah Flagg prodded sharply, 'that you wasn't here when it happened—that you come along later?'

The prisoner eased breath from his lungs. 'You might take a look at these tracks,' he said, reaching for any plausible-sounding argument. 'Must have been four or five in the bunch that done this, and they're long since gone. If I'd been one of them, does it make sense that I'd stay around—or come back, after the others left?'

It didn't sound too strong an argument, even as he gave it, but it seemed to have effect. The marks of the horses were plain enough, in mud around the spring. He watched the Flaggs studying them, and for the first time saw a flicker of doubt come into their hostile faces. As usual, they waited for Noah's decision; after a moment the old man tilted his head—the barest hint of a nod.

31

'All right, Wheelock,' he said grudgingly, and the latter felt his nerves begin to loosen. 'I guess that sort of puts you in the clear. If I really thought you was holding out on me—that you maybe knew more than you're telling ... Well, you better not!'

Wheelock didn't bat an eye. 'I can't say I blame you for that.' He looked at the body on the ground. 'He was your son?'

The old man nodded again. 'These boys with me are some his brothers, some his cousins. And us Flaggs are closer than a lot of families,' he said bleakly. 'We know who our enemies are. We'll find which ones done this, and we'll settle with them—every last man. You just better hope you wasn't one of them!'

'I believe you!' Burn Wheelock said.

But the immediate threat seemed to have lifted. He was breathing more easily. Not wanting to press his luck, he asked, 'Can I go now?' and got a curt nod from the old man, who dismissed him without so much as a look. He tried not to appear in too much haste as he turned away to his horse, got the stirrup, and swung astride. More than one of the Flaggs were watching him narrowly but no one spoke, no one seemed inclined to stop him.

Wheelock swung around them and rode on out of the hollow. By the time he had put a couple of miles behind him, the queasy uneasiness had begun to settle somewhat.

As the sound of the stranger's leaving threaded out into the stillness of the hollow, Mason Flagg said darkly, 'We should have held onto him, Pa. I still think he lied to you.'

'He was a nobody,' Noah Flagg retorted. 'A damned drifter. We know it was one of the big outfits that killed Rufe—Y-Bar, or one of them others that's been wanting to see us run out of Oregon if they could. Don't worry—we'll find out which!' He added, 'Now, some of you boys get down there and help Homer put Rufe on his saddle.'

The old man watched with bitter eyes as this was done—gnarled, liver-spotted hands piled on the saddlehorn, unmoving except for the faint stirring of his jaws. When the dead man had been lifted across the back of his horse and lashed in place, one of the younger men asked, 'We gonna bury him in the Antelope cemetery, Pa?'

'Damn right!' Noah Flagg leaned to deposit a brown stain of juice on the ground beside his horse's front leg. 'In the fanciest coffin we can find in that town: silk lining, brass handles— the works. We'll go in now and arrange it. Quincy'—and his keen glance singled out one of the clan—'you better ride on home and tell the wimmen folks. Have 'em get his good suit brushed and ready to lay him out in.'

The one so delegated left obediently on his

33

errand. Mason Flagg walked over to his father; he was holding a short length of yellow hemp, with the noose and the bulky hangman's knot fashioned in one end of it, that he must have hacked off the rope taken from his brother's body. 'Here's what they hanged him with,' he said grimly. 'Take a look at it, Pa. You see what I see?'

Noah scowled as he accepted the ugly thing. 'Rope looks new.'

'Brand new, Pa! Just bought recent, I'll wager, and never been used before. And ain't that some kind of clue for us? If we's to lean on 'em a little, ain't one of them storekeepers in Antelope just apt to be able to tell us the name of the man he sold this to?'

Eyes glittering with pale fire behind their narrowed lids, Noah Flagg slowly nodded. 'By God, son, that's usin' your head!' He slapped the noose sharply against a knee. 'That's usin' it damn good! With this,' he promised, 'we'll git the truth out of them town people! We'll learn which outfit murdered your brother— and then, hell itself cain't stop us evenin' the score . . .'

*   *   *

Fred Adler had been around this section of Oregon as long as anyone—though actually, that would have been a matter of less than twenty years—and when he built he had built

34

for staying. His house was a low-roofed, sprawling structure of stone and log, with a chimney of lava rock at one end and wooden shutters at the windows that must have proved handy in the early days, against Snake Indian raiders. There were juniper-pole corrals, a well with a sweep, and a barn of the same construction as the house.

A glow of approaching sunset softened the rude contours of the place as Burn Wheelock rode in, following the wagon road he had picked up out on the open flats. Blue smoke drifted from the stone chimney's mouth, and as Wheelock looked around him a man came from the barn carrying some harness over his shoulder. He gave the stranger a look that seemed oddly hostile.

Wheelock greeted him civilly enough. 'This the Adler place?'

'He ain't here!' the other grunted.

He was not only unfriendly, he struck Wheelock as not particularly bright. Slightly puzzled, the latter was framing a second question when they were interrupted by a call from over at the house. Turning, Wheelock saw Fred Adler himself standing on the porch, his gray head bared and an apron tied around his gaunt middle. 'George?' he called. 'Anything wrong?'

'Nothing wrong, Mr Adler,' Burn Wheelock answered, before the scowling George could speak. He kneed his horse and rode over

35

toward the house, and saw recognition in the rancher's dark and wrinkled face. Adler seemed pleased to see him.

'It is you,' he said, in a voice that held strong echoes of his native German speech. 'Welcome, friend. I was cooking supper. You will join us.'

'Thanks,' Wheelock said as he dismounted. He couldn't help adding, 'Your man, there, didn't sound as though I'd be too welcome.'

'George you must not mind,' the other told him. 'He's only jealous, of his job. He thinks you might be looking for work, and I might hire you.'

Wheelock paused, in the act of wrapping his reins to a roof post. 'You ain't hiring, then? You got all the crew you need?'

'Not all I need, but all I can afford—after the winter we are getting through by the skin of our teeth! The cattle I managed to save, George and I can handle after a fashion. As for George, he is a little dumb in the head, yah; but he does the best he can. I think it is only right I should keep him.'

'Sure,' Burn Wheelock said gruffly, unable to keep the disappointment from showing. 'Well, I won't lie to you. I did come looking for work. You'd said, when I talked to you before—'

Faded blue eyes frowned at him, puzzled. 'But I am thinking, you work for Harper Youngdahl. Just the other day I see him, and

36

he has said you are making a good hand for him.'

'I had to quit ... something came up. Well, I'm sorry to have bothered you...' He didn't want to get involved in explanations, and there was no reason to stay longer. He started to reach for the stirrup.

'But you are staying for supper,' the rancher protested. 'Let me check my biscuits, and we will talk some more.'

Wheelock followed him inside the house. Adler had never married and he batched it here with whatever crew he had. There was a single room with three tiers of bunks built against the walls, only a couple of them holding ticks and blankets now. Wheelock slacked into a chair and placed his hat on the table, watching while his host worked at the deep stone fireplace— stirring a pot of stew on the crane, lifting the lid of a Dutch oven buried in the coals. The aroma of food set the juices flowing in the young man's mouth. He had been too upset to realize he was so hungry.

Adler brought over the iron coffeepot and filled a cup for him, and watched him as he drank it. He shook his head. 'I am thinking it is not easy, to be finding another job just now.'

'I wouldn't be surprised,' Wheelock said. 'I know the score.'

The old man rubbed his jaw. 'You are seeing perhaps Bill Pitcher? Or Masters, at the Rafter M? Besides Youngdahl, these are the only two

37

I know who may be able to hire—if they have not already all the help they need.'

'Thanks. I hoped maybe you'd suggest somebody,' Wheelock admitted over the rim of the cup. 'If you can tell me how to find these people, I'll sure give them a try.'

'It's only a chance. There are of course some sheep outfits, over toward Cross Hollows...'

Wheelock made a face. 'I ain't come to *that* yet. I'd rather try another range.'

Adler turned back to his cooking. 'You will stay the night with us. This food is being ready when you have finished your coffee and taken care of your horse.'

Wheelock was graining his roan when George came stalking into the barn. His manner was still so glumly suspicious that Wheelock couldn't resist telling him, 'Look! You can take that chip off your shoulder! Adler's already said he ain't hiring anybody, so your job is safe. I'll be gone by morning.' George blinked at him, vacant-eyed. Burn Wheelock shrugged and gave up on him.

Supper was brief and matter-of-fact. After Wheelock had helped clean up, in return for his meal, George got out a checkerboard and men for what apparently was the usual evening routine. But Adler claimed to be in no mood for a game; he wanted to talk, and he summoned Wheelock, with a jerk of his head, out onto the porch. There they sat on the steps and he lit up a pipe; the two looked in silence awhile, at the bright mesh of stars that curved down beyond the rim-rock. The tang of tobacco smoke was sharp against the wild smells of springtime.

'You wish to talk about it?' the old man asked suddenly.

Startled, Wheelock said, 'About what?'

'This I am not knowing. But I think it is something more than being out of work. I think it is not new to you, riding the grubline ... Were you having a quarrel with Youngdahl? Or perhaps'—he corrected himself, his tone edged with dislike—'that Jess Croy...' Burn Wheelock wondered if the sudden start he gave was visible in the darkness, because the old man added, with a sound that was almost like a chuckle, 'I think now I am guessing well.'

'I—' The younger man floundered, and faltered. And then—perhaps because it had been bottled up too long—something brought it tumbling out. 'A man was hanged today. I—' He started to say, 'I was there,' but at the last minute changed that to: 'I found the body.'

'I see.' Adler behaved as though that explained a lot. He drew deep on the pipe, so that its reddish glow fanned up across his expressionless mouth and cheeks. 'Bad,' he said finally. 'Very bad for a young man who is not ever being involved in such things before.'

Wheelock looked at him sharply. 'You sound like it wouldn't bother *you* too much.

Maybe you even been involved sometime, yourself!'

'That,' the old man replied blandly, 'I won't say. But I have been around—I am living a long time. I understand these things.'

'You approve of a man executing his personal enemies?' the younger man demanded angrily. 'Taking it on himself—like he was the law, or God, or somebody?'

'Of course not. But the West has always been hanging its own horse thieves and rustlers and the like, and not too much thinking about lawbooks. The country is too big. Wasco County is too big. They are carving it up, lately, but still too much is left. Law and order, they spread thin here.'

Wheelock said, 'I've heard talk about a new sheriff at The Dalles. Supposed to be pretty tough...'

'"Tough,"' the old German echoed. 'Yah! This is Sam Rankin. He is wishing to build respect for the law in Wasco County—and I think he will not mind to break a few heads if he must. It is necessary to take this Sheriff Rankin very much into account.' Adler stretched out an arm and knocked the dottle from his pipe against a roof support; sparks went streaming on the night wind, that had risen as darkness settled. He said, almost casually, 'You were not mentioning just who it was got hanged.'

'I guess I didn't. It was a man named Rufe Flagg.'

40

That got a low, thoughtful whistle. 'Flagg!' Fred Adler echoed softly. 'Now I see...'

'You don't sound too surprised. Maybe you expected something like this?'

'One hears things,' the other admitted. After a moment he added, 'I have a bad feeling. Those people of his will never let it go. And they are the kind who would be picking an enemy off from around a rock!'

'Is that a warning?' Burn Wheelock demanded, past the solid lump in his throat.

'Should it be?' The rancher gave him a shrewd look. 'You say you found the body. Is that really all you had to do with it? If not, you are perhaps lucky you *don't* find another job. Other places could be more healthy for you...'

'Oh well,' Wheelock said, and shrugged. 'Sooner or later other places generally begin to look better to me.'

The older man told him slowly, 'That is sad, too. I am not much older than you, I think, when I come to this country in '48—across an ocean, from a Germany where we are trying to win freedom, only to have our Revolution put down in pain and blood...'

In the darkness, Fred Adler's voice held tragic memory. 'Is not good, always wandering. Someday you will know...' Then, his tone abruptly changing: 'The death of Rufe Flagg ... is this by chance anything to do with the reason you leave Y-Bar?'

'You ask too many questions!' Wheelock
41

said gruffly, and got to his feet. 'Far as I'm concerned it's a closed issue.' Or so at least he hoped—but then he thought of the mad glitter in Noah Flagg's wall-eyed stare, and he suppressed a shudder. He heard himself muttering: 'Getting sort of chilly out here, don't you reckon?'

'If you say.' On that, the talk ended.

CHAPTER FOUR

Antelope was trying hard to be a town.

Twenty years ago—back in the days of the rush to the John Day goldfields and of the marauding raids by the Snake chief, Paulina—there had been Howard Maupin's station on the stage road from The Dalles to Canyon City. Maupin had long since left for other parts. Then, a couple of years back, the stageline shifted its route to a crossing a mile or so farther down Antelope Creek, and the new station owner had moved his business there. A townsite had been started. The stage station and post office; a couple of stores; a couple of saloons; a hotel and a blacksmith shop and an all-purpose building that had come to be known as 'Tammany Hall'—this was about all there was, so far, to this town scattered along its single street, where Antelope Valley gentled out before narrowing to become a lava-

42

rimmed canyon, farther downstream.

Burn Wheelock rode in, toward noon of the day after Rufe Flagg's hanging and of his own visit to Fred Adler. He had been here twice before, briefly, during his short stay in the Central Oregon country; he knew no one at all, but it was a place where he could buy trail rations. And that was what he had in mind because he was leaving, Adler's prediction having been proved exactly right: There simply was no work for a grubliner, not on this range and not this season. So he had learned at the Masters spread, and he had been spared a useless ride to see the other rancher Adler had mentioned since Masters knew, for a fact, that Bill Pitcher wasn't hiring either.

His fruitless quest having brought him within a few miles of Antelope which was the hub for this sparsely settled stretch of bunch grass range, it was obvious that the next move was to pick up a few supplies for his saddlebags, to sustain him while he traveled to whatever place he would try next.

Spring was the changeable season, here in the rain shadow of the Cascades. Yesterday had all been clear, warm sunshine; this morning, a gray cloudsheet rested on the lava rims and there were a few stinging spears of rain in the wind that scoured the dusty street. The wind had probably driven the life of the town indoors, but there wasn't much activity here at any time. As he was dismounting at

Bowers's Mercantile, Wheelock noticed an unexpected number of horses tied in front of a saloon at the street's end and looked at them narrowly.

One, he thought, resembled the bigheaded dun he had seen Noah Flagg riding yesterday. Burn Wheelock wanted no more to do with any of that family. That he had seen the last of them was one of the compensations for admitting defeat, and leaving this country forever— taking little with him except a few dollars in his pocket, and a jaw that still ached from the blow with Jess Croy's gun barrel.

He walked into the store and found its owner fussing around, grumpily straightening out the merchandise on his tables that seemed to have got badly scrambled. Balding, and nearsighted in octagonal spectacles, he didn't seem to remember Wheelock from the other time he'd been in. There was something overwrought and tense about him, as he peered at his customer and demanded, 'You here for the buryin'?'

'Buryin'?' Wheelock repeated. 'Not that I'm aware of.'

'Thought for a minute you might be one of them Flaggs.' Wheelock thought the man sounded highly relieved that he wasn't. He went on, 'I suppose you heard about Rufe?'

'I heard something,' Wheelock said carefully.

'They planted him this morning. The whole

44

outfit was in town for it—wagonloads of them. Their women, too: They came flocking in afterward to paw over my stock but nobody bought anything at all. I doubt those people let their womenfolk see two bits, in hard cash, from one year's end to another. They damn well don't know what to do with themselves, inside a store!' He shook his head as he laboriously finished rerolling a bolt of cheap cloth someone had unwound and left spilled in a heap.

Burn Wheelock was prompted to remark, 'I hear somebody strung Rufe Flagg up to a tree. Do they know yet who might have done that?'

'Not as I've heard. But you can bet his kin ain't going to let it drop. A bunch of them are still down at Silvertooth's—having them a regular wake, I understand.'

So that explained the lineup of horses outside the saloon. Burn Wheelock made note of that—decided that he might be well advised to get his supplies purchased, and leave. He told the storekeeper what he needed—some airtights, coffee, dried beans, tobacco, a small bag of salt and one of sugar. The man left off tidying his stock long enough to fill the order; only one item proved beyond him. 'I'm all out of smoking,' he said. 'You might try across the street.'

'All right.'

Waiting to have his purchases stowed into a gunnysack, he ranged a glance over the store's

45

interior and saw, hanging on the rear partition, some 35-foot coils of yellow hemp—a standard length for the cattle country. They reminded him of a need he had forgotten and without thinking he told the storekeeper, 'Oh, yeah. I'll want one of them ropes...'

Everything seemed to stop. The other man looked at the pale yellow coils on their spikes, and then again at his customer, and there was an expression behind the nearsighted stare that had not been there before. Burn Wheelock all at once felt his mouth go dry as he wondered if he had, inadvertently, made some terrible and stupid mistake. But he bluffed it through, boldly returning the proprietor's look until the man turned away to fetch the rope.

When he brought it back he slapped it down on the counter with more force than seemed necessary. Burn Wheelock had his money ready. 'I guess that ought to do it,' he said, easily enough. 'How much?' He counted it out, took his change and his purchases. The parting nod he gave received no answer at all.

He had no sooner walked outside, than the door shut behind him and he heard, distinctly, the turning of a key in the lock. He turned and frowned at the door, for a long moment. But then he remembered it was close to noon. 'Likely in a hurry to get home to dinner,' Wheelock said aloud. Still, he had an uneasy feeling as he returned to his waiting horse.

His impulse was to mount and ride, but he

46

made himself take his time about putting his purchases away in the saddlebags. Afterward, on the chance he was being watched, he took his animal by the reins and led him across the wind-swept street, as though only interested in trying somewhere else for smoking tobacco.

*   *   *

Nate Bowers lost no time. Having all but slammed the door on his departing customer, he was careful to leave by the rear entrance and use the weed-grown alleyway behind the store, not making his way back to the street, and across it, until he had come opposite the Union Hotel. He was a little breathless when he entered the lobby and asked the man behind the desk, 'Is Rankin here?'

'Just checked back in, maybe a half hour ago,' the clerk told him. 'Room seven, front. Anything wrong, Nate?'

Bowers had no time to answer questions. He hurried up the stairs, and along the corridor that still had some of the new smell of raw lumber, the hotel like the town itself being no more than a couple of years old. At number seven he knocked and heard an abrupt command to enter.

The room's occupant had been washing up in the china bowl on the commode. Water glistened in his thick mane of reddish hair, as Sam Rankin tossed aside the towel and

47

reached for a clean shirt hung over the foot of the brass bedstead; he looked at his visitor as he pulled it on and began to work with the buttons. 'Well,' he said sourly, 'I guess they got him planted.'

The storekeeper, still breathless, nodded.

'I've been out to take a look at where he was hanged,' the sheriff continued. 'Not much to see, after the way they messed up the sign.'

Rankin's voice had a permanent edge—the tired disgust of one who had put up with too much weakness and too much stupidity in lesser men. It was this intolerance, and a kind of inner intensity that seemed to have eaten away any scrap of spare flesh from his ruddy, wind-roughened cheeks, that made him seem older than forty-five. Deep lines bracketed a thin-lipped and bitter mouth. Eyes of an odd tawny color centered on the other man suddenly, seeming to notice his excitement. 'What's the matter with *you*?'

Nate Bowers had got some of his breath back. His glance shifted to the bed and to the hacked-off length of rope, in the shape of a noose and hangman's knot, that hung over one of its knobs. 'Sheriff, I've found the answer you and the Flaggs have both been looking for. I think I know where that came from.'

'I've known all along where it came from,' the lawman answered. 'Right out of your store.'

The merchant acknowledged this with an

48

inclination of his head. 'You were right ... Just now a man came in and bought some things. He looked vaguely familiar but I really didn't place him—not until he asked for rope. And then it struck me.'

Rankin's hands, working with the shirt buttons, had gone still. His strange eyes bored into the other. 'So?'

'It must have been two weeks ago. The same man was in and bought a rope from me. A hat, too, as I remember. He was with Harper Youngdahl.'

The sheriff had been nodding, as though pleased at this confirmation of a hunch. But now his head jerked and the eyes went hard. '*Youngdahl!* You're sure?'

'Of course. He—'

A hand shot out, seized the other in a grip that made him wince. 'You'd better be *damned* sure! Don't make any mistake on this!'

Bowers had paled a little, under the punishment of that hand on his shoulder. 'I'm telling you what happened,' he exclaimed. 'I stood in the door and watched the two of them ride away together. I got the impression this fellow had just hired on.'

The sheriff let him go, but he swore harshly and bitterly. 'You understand what it means. If somebody like Youngdahl's mixed up in this, then anything can come of it!' He added, 'Where is the man you're talking about?'

Before answering, Bowers moved hurriedly

49

to the window. It was a corner window, offering a good view along the dusty street below. 'That's him!' The storekeeper pointed. 'I remember, he said he had to look for some tobacco...'

Rankin joined him and they looked at the man who stood beside his waiting horse, rolling up a cigarette. The sheriff said testily, 'I don't know why you weren't able to remember any of this before.'

The merchant lifted his shoulders. 'With both you and the Flaggs putting on the pressure? I think, between you, you scared it right out of my head!'

The point didn't seem worth arguing. Sheriff Rankin had turned away, to snatch up a corduroy jacket that had his badge of office pinned to the lapel. He shrugged into it, took his hat and, as an afterthought, the noose hanging on the bedpost. At the door he paused to pin the other man with a hard look. 'Not a word of this to anyone. Especially not the Flaggs. You understand me?'

Nate Bowers nodded quickly. 'Of course. Not a word!' The sheriff swung away, leaving the door open, and went tramping with firm purpose along the uncarpeted hallway toward the stairs, not waiting for the slower-moving storekeeper.

The first match Burn Wheelock had struck sputtered out when a gust of wind caught it. He dropped it into the dirt, brought out another and snapped it to life and shielded it with his palms until he had the paper burning and got the first taste of tobacco smoke in his mouth. Afterward he stepped around his horse and was about to free the reins when he became aware of someone approaching. Luckily it wasn't a Flagg; nonetheless, something in the look of him suggested he meant serious business, and Wheelock left the reins alone and waited.

All at once he asked himself why he couldn't have left this town, while he had a clear field. Now it just might be too late.

Then he caught the glint of metal on the other's coat front. A badge ... He wasn't aware that Antelope boasted any sort of formal law; it was another moment before it occurred to him this might be the tough sheriff from The Dalles, himself. He kept his face expressionless as the man came to a halt in front of him.

He was no more than medium height—perhaps even an inch less than Burn Wheelock, who was not a tall man. But there was a compact intensity about him that impressed you—a forcefulness, in the energy he seemed to exude. He was carrying something, but the skirt of his unbuttoned coat, flapping in the gusty wind, partially hid it.

'My name's Rankin,' the stranger announced without preliminary. 'Sheriff of this county. I'd like a word with you.'

'Why me?'

'I think you know,' the sheriff answered bluntly. 'And if you're smart, you'll give me true answers. First off, I want your name.'

The young man gave it, and saw Rankin's stare betray a start of surprise.

'*You're* Wheelock?' he echoed, and added grimly, 'Now I *know* I want to talk to you!' Just then a particularly hard gust of wind pummeled them, stinging them with grit and needles of cold rain and causing them both to stagger. The roan shifted its hoofs and Sam Rankin said, 'I think we'd best get under a roof...'

The yawning doorway of a livery barn stood open, not many yards distant; reluctantly, Wheelock took his animal by its reins and followed the other there. They stood within the entrance, amid the smells of old hay and horses and mice, but sheltered from the tearing gusts of gritty wind.

And for the first time Burn Wheelock saw clearly what it was the sheriff had in his hand, and he felt his throat go dry. Rankin caught this reaction. He held up the ugly noose and said, 'You've seen this before, I guess.'

'I guess those Flaggs give it to you,' Wheelock suggested.

'That's right.' The sheriff nodded. 'I came down on the stage from The Dalles yesterday, to serve some tax papers. I'd no more than lit when old Noah Flagg brought in his son's body. He told me a man with your name was there when they found him, hanging.'

'Yes, and I explained about that.'

'You didn't explain about it being your rope he was hanged with!' When he saw the other hesitate over an answer, the sheriff went on bluntly: 'Nate Bowers has identified you as the man who bought it from him—right over there in his store, two weeks ago.'

Burn Wheelock thought he could feel the waters rising about his throat, as he saw how deeply he was getting embroiled—all because of a moment's foolish error. Whatever had he been thinking of, to point a finger at himself by insisting on buying another rope? It could just as easily have waited till he reached some other place...

He tried to settle his breathing. It seemed the time to try a bluff, however futile, and he pointed out, 'A rope's not as easy to identify as a man, Sheriff. One looks about like another. I don't think anybody could say for sure this is the one I bought.'

'Oh?' The eyes were hard as iron. 'Then where *is* the one you bought?'

Wheelock swallowed. He couldn't quite meet the challenge of those strange tawny eyes, and he dropped his own as he said, without conviction, 'Looks as though I lost it.'

'Lost it around Rufe Flagg's neck?' Rankin made an ugly sound. 'Now you listen to me!' he went on sternly. 'You can make things just as tough on yourself as you like. Or, you can use

53

your head and quit covering up.'

'Covering up?' the young fellow echoed. 'For who?'

'Your boss. Youngdahl.'

Burn Wheelock could only stare, in the gloomy silence of the barn. There seemed *nothing* he could hide from this man ... At that moment the rain began—hard, drifting in silver sheets before the wind, pelting the dirt street into an instant quagmire. The smell of wet earth surrounded them.

The racket of the downpour was so loud Wheelock had to raise his voice against it. 'You seem to think you know a helluva lot about me!'

'I think I do,' Sam Rankin answered, with cold and irritating smugness. 'You work for Harper Youngdahl. A saddle rope belonging to you was used for stringing up Rufe Flagg. If not by you personally—and I'm willing to give you the benefit of that doubt, because somehow you don't look the type—then by Youngdahl or some of his crew. I suppose they caught him running off some Y-Bar stuff?'

All the younger man could muster was, 'You're guessing!'

'Knowing the Flaggs, it's pretty obvious.'

'Then, if you know that about 'em,' Wheelock retorted, 'why haven't you done something? Why are they left loose, to run off other men's cattle?'

For a moment he thought the sheriff was

54

going to hit him, but then some of the anger smoothed out of Rankin's craggy face and he nodded slowly. 'You got a fair question,' the lawman admitted, 'and the answer is that I lack the proof, and the manpower. It's a big county—a damn sight too big, for the kind of force the sheriff's office can muster on the budget I'm allowed. One of these days, I'll nail that crowd; but for the time being'—and his voice toughened—'I will not stand for any more of what happened yesterday!

'Men on the frontier have been thinking too long they had the right—or some kind of duty even—to take on the law's functions. Maybe, one time, that sort of thing was justified; but the time's past. And while I'm sheriff of this county, there's going to be none of it here. None!'

As he spoke the words, a kind of furious intensity sparked those strangely colored eyes. It occurred to Burn Wheelock that, on this one subject, he was dealing with a determined and dangerous man—one just as fanatic as Noah Flagg himself. He felt uncomfortably the need to make some answer. 'Nobody's saying you're wrong,' he muttered.

'Then will you help me? Are you willing to talk?'

But the young man shook his head doggedly. 'I thought I made it clear. I admit I bought a rope from Bowers, but I don't admit it's the one you've got in your hand. And that's all I'm going to say.'

Wind through the wide doorway blew a spray of chill rain in at them. The lawman's face had darkened. The hand that held the noose lifted now and it was trembling with anger. He let it drop to his side again and he said tightly: 'What is it? Have they got you scared to open your mouth? Or'—his eyes narrowed slightly—'is it some dumb idea about loyalty to whatever outfit you happen to ride for?'

Something he read in Wheelock's silence must have convinced him. Scorn entered his tone. 'You better get *that* out of your head, because there's no truth in it! Harper Youngdahl ain't a bad man, by his lights. But just because you draw his pay, is no proper reason to put yourself out on a limb ... Dammit, are you listening to me?'

As the sheriff's anger grew, a kind of stubbornness had settled in Burn Wheelock. He shook his head, his face expressionless. 'I'm listening. And I've said all I intend to.'

Sam Rankin swore fiercely. 'All right,' he snapped. 'I guess I know my next move. Youngdahl's expected to show up in town sometime this afternoon, to get his mail. I'll take the matter up with him. Meanwhile, *you're* not through yet! I can tell you now, if this town had a jail you'd be in it!'

'Because of a lousy piece of rope?' Wheelock retorted bitterly. 'That you can't prove was

56

mine?'

'I don't have to prove it—at the very least you're a material witness.' Rankin laid a warning finger against the other's chest. 'So just don't try to leave, Wheelock, before I say you can. I'll take it as an admission of guilt. I'll come after you, and drag you back—and there'll be enough to see that *you* hang, whether I get Youngdahl or not. You better believe that!'

He punctuated the warning with a hard stab of the finger, that actually drove the young fellow back a step. Not giving Wheelock time to answer, the sheriff turned and put a shout into the gloom of the barn: 'Anybody on duty here? Speak up!'

The door of a tack room creaked open; a man put his head out and then diffidently followed it. He was bony, ageless in soiled bib overalls; he shifted his stare uneasily from one to the other as he shuffled forward. 'Who are you?' Sam Rankin demanded.

'Cooley, Sheriff. Joe Cooley—day hostler.'

'All right, Cooley.' The lawman indicated Burn Wheelock who stood speechless, slowly rubbing his chest where the finger had prodded him. 'This man wants to put his horse up. The charges are to go on the county bill. You got that clear?'

'Yes, sir.'

The sheriff nodded. He gave Burn Wheelock a final look, full of warning. After that Rankin spun on his heel and walked out of the barn, and the young man watched him go—a compact and restless figure, shouldering through the thin rain as though it were a physical barrier.

CHAPTER FIVE

Burn Wheelock shook free, with an effort, from the impact of so much will and energy. Turning he saw the hostler watching him uncertainly, a hand outstretched for the reins. He shrugged and passed them over.

'All right,' he said heavily. 'If it's on the county, I might as well have you go ahead and give him a graining.' He added, 'Don't bother taking off the saddle! It ain't sure how long I'll be here.'

'But I thought the sheriff said—' Cooley broke off there. The other's sharp look must have decided him that it was all none of his business, for he simply ducked his head, leaving the words unfinished, and turned away with the roan in tow.

Burn Wheelock stopped him with a question. 'Where's a place to get a meal in this town?' Since he was to be held here, he told himself he could at least put the time lost to some use.

The hostler gave him a look across a
58

shoulder. 'Hotel's as good as any, I guess.' Wheelock thanked him with a nod, and heard the thud of the roan's shoes on hard-packed dirt as the man led it farther into the shadows of the barn.

He stepped again into the doorway, to take a look at the rain-swept village.

The storm was already easing and wouldn't last long. Flipping up his collar, he set out along the street that had been converted into black mud, with standing puddles whose surfaces were flecked by the spears of rain.

On the steps of the Union Hotel he took off his hat and swatted it against his leg, to dislodge the few drops it had collected. Entering, he passed through the empty lobby and into the dining room that was equally empty. He took a table near a window and placed his hat on the floor beside his chair. Early as it was, he supposed he was the first customer; to the man who came from the kitchen he said gruffly, 'Bring me whatever you got.'

'You just ordered stew,' the man said, and left him to his worries.

Except for his own stupidity, by this time he could already have been on his way out of this country; now, thanks to Sheriff Rankin, he'd lost the chance. Burn Wheelock scowled at the drops of water rattling like buckshot against the window pane. He couldn't remember being this scared and depressed before, in his life.

Having just paid a visit to Silvertooth's outhouse, Mason Flagg was on his way back inside when someone hailed him. It was Joe Cooley, the livery stable hostler.

'You got something on your mind?' Flagg demanded.

Cooley glanced quickly around, as though uneasy about being seen. Plainly though he was bursting to tell his news: 'I thought you'd be wanting to know what I heard just now, at the barn—between the sheriff and that fellow Wheelock...'

The bigger man eyed him impatiently. 'Well?' But by the time Cooley was finished, Flagg's whole manner had changed; he made the hostler back up and tell it all again—every word that had been spoken, from the moment the two men had walked into the stable.

He was smoldering with anger, his pale eyes glittering. 'So that sonofabitch Wheelock had the nerve to lie to us. Not a grubliner—a *Youngdahl* man! And that was his own Goddamn rope!' Mason Flagg cursed, an explosive sound. 'Even Nate Bowers lied— swearin' up and down he didn't know anything! The Flaggs may just have to pay that store-keeper another visit,' he suggested ominously. 'After we get through with Wheelock. Where is he now, do you know?'

Sensing the danger in the man, Cooley

60

stammered out his answer. 'Wheelock? Why, after Rankin gave him orders not to leave town, he asked me where to eat and I suggested the hotel dining room. He may be there, having dinner.'

'I hope he enjoys it,' Flagg said harshly, showing all his teeth in a cruel grin; and with that he turned on his heel and headed quickly for the saloon's rear door, to join his relatives.

The hostler called after him anxiously, 'You wouldn't let on to the sheriff or anyone, that it was me—?' But Flagg hadn't even heard him.

Overhead a single streak of dazzle seamed the cloud cover, where the sun appeared to be trying to come through.

*   *   *

Tom Shecky, following his boss and the foreman into town, saw that bright streak widen and run like cracks in a plate, as clouds began to pull apart. Color came back into the world and steam wavered in streamers, where sunlight shafted through to strike the soaked ground. Almost at once, his yellow slicker became unbearably warm and he stripped out of it, shook it out and laid it across the saddle in front of him. Raw odors of wet earth and sage and timber were pleasant after the brief storm. But Tom Shecky wasn't too much aware of them.

Even now, a full day later, he was still shaken
61

to the core by the execution of Rufe Flagg, turned nearly ill at the thought of his own part in it. That he'd only followed orders might be some comfort, if it weren't for the example of that fellow Wheelock who had refused to follow them—showing, instead, the temerity to stand up to Jess Croy and nearly get his skull cracked open. It was bitter to know he, himself, lacked that kind of courage; still, under the goading of a man as rough and determined as the Y-Bar foreman it wasn't always easy to keep your head, or to remember that even if you were only a hired hand, you were supposed to have a will, and a conscience, of your own.

Up ahead, now, he could see the wet roofs of the town shining in the sun like mirrors. With the ending of the rain, the foreman had peeled out of his own slicker and now Harper Youngdahl shed the black rubber poncho he favored. Looking at the backs of these two men who were his bosses, Tom Shecky was all too conscious of the tight-mouthed silence between them.

No one had spoken a word, during the ride in from the ranch; there was bad feeling there, and no one had to tell him the reason for the brooding displeasure Harper Youngdahl was showing toward his foreman.

As they reached the stage station at the upper end of the street, Shecky said to break the silence, 'I'll check the mail.' Youngdahl, still scowling, did no more than nod. Shecky thought the other two would ride on, but they reined in as he dismounted—plainly, they intended to wait. He left his slicker hanging on the saddlehorn, and walked inside the station.

It was Antelope's post office, as well. Just now the door to the agent's cubicle, and the mail room, was tight shut and locked. Tom Shecky knocked and called out but got no answer. He turned to leave the building, then, meaning to tell the others he would hang around until the agent returned and join them later, when he had collected the mail.

Outside he came abruptly to a halt.

From the doorway he saw at once he had stumbled into the midst of something. Youngdahl and Croy were as he had left them, but they had moved their horses around to face a man who stood in the puddled street, confronting them with his head tilted back and the weak sunlight showing the wind-whipped planes of a ruddy face. Shecky had never met the sheriff of Wasco County; it was the badge on his coat identified him. Sam Rankin looked angry, and Harper Youngdahl's face too appeared tight and grim.

Oddly, the Y-Bar foreman was the one doing the talking: 'Rufe Flagg was born to hang— just like all the rest of 'em. But does that bastard, Wheelock, claim *we* done it? If he does he's lying. Let him dare say it to my face!'

Harper Youngdahl shifted on the saddle and shook his head as he spoke reprovingly. 'Now,

63

let's not fly off the handle. I just don't think young Wheelock would have said anything of the sort.' He put his deliberate gaze on the sheriff and the latter lifted a shoulder, shrugging.

'No, as a matter of fact he ain't saying much of anything—he's stubborn.' Rankin wagged his head. 'But, he can break! I just wondered if you had anything you might want to tell me, first—before I really go to work on him.'

'I had better not hear of you getting tough with that young fellow, Rankin!' the rancher answered crisply. 'He's a good man.'

'But you told me he quit you. Are you willing yet to tell me why?'

Without hesitation Youngdahl shook his head. 'That's between us.'

'Then you'll do nothing to help the law in this matter?' The sheriff's thick chest swelled with a breath; he seemed, in his anger, to grow inches taller. 'All right! I'll get to the bottom of it—in spite of you, if I have to. And I won't forget!'

That seemed to end it. No one answered and the sheriff swung away as though he had no more to add, but after a couple of steps he appeared to remember something else and turned back. 'I almost forgot to say, the Flaggs are still in town. I don't want any trouble— deliberate, or by accident. You understand me?'

Jess Croy swelled a little and Shecky thought

64

the foreman was going to give vent to more of his bluster. But something cooled him; silently, they all watched Sam Rankin plow across the muddy street with that intent, energetic prowl of his, and climb the steps to the hotel veranda.

Under his breath, Croy muttered something.

'That'll do!' Harper Youngdahl's tone silenced him, and whipped his head around. 'Sam Rankin is trying, without anybody's help, to win some kind of respect for the law in this county. I just wish to God I *could* help him—because he's right, and this time I'm wrong!'

Croy's face darkened. 'You wouldn't be thinking of turning me over to him?'

For a long moment the two men shared an angry look. Then Harper Youngdahl wearily shook his head as he lifted the reins. 'No,' he said, 'I'm not turning you over to him.' To Tom Shecky, he appeared a discouraged and disheartened man.

*　　　　*　　　　*

Burn Wheelock, with his dinner half-eaten and the rest of it growing cold on his plate, had had a view of that scene from the dining-room window. He ran the window up, but the distance was too great for voices to carry above the noise of water runneling, in a shining rope, from a hole in the gutter. He stood frowning and tried to judge what was going on in front of

65

the stage station.

Then he saw Sam Rankin turn and start in his direction, heading directly toward the hotel, and he felt a twinge of alarm. The sheriff's destination might be one of the upstairs rooms; but on the other hand he could be on his way to the dining room, and Wheelock suddenly knew he didn't want another confrontation—at least, not knowing what had been said just now, out there on the street. Quickly he turned from the window, pausing at his table to drop silver beside his plate and pick his hat from the floor. The dining room had an outside door onto the street. He went and opened this.

Keeping out of sight, he waited until the sheriff had mounted the lobby steps and passed beyond his range of vision. Stepping out, then, he closed the door behind him and drew on his hat. He ran a palm nervously across his jaws, debating whether to go out and talk to Youngdahl right then or perhaps wait for a chance to see him alone, without needing to have further dealings with Jess Croy. And in that moment of uncertainty he heard, faintly to his left, a man's voice that yelled, 'Ain't that him?'

His head jerked around. The sun had broken free of the tattered clouds now and every wet surface of street and buildings made a bright dazzle, but he could distinguish the shapes of two men standing in the weedy path that did duty for a sidewalk. Silvertooth's saloon was just beyond, and Burn Wheelock knew at once that he had been discovered by the Flaggs.

Suddenly those two began running toward him. He saw flashes of metal as one of the pair brought up a gun from behind his waist belt; that jarred him free, and sent him whirling again toward the closed door. He groped for the knob, had a moment's trouble turning it with a palm that was suddenly wet with sweat. Just as he got the door wrenched open, a gunshot sounded upon the street's quiet; a bullet slapped into the wood of the jamb, missing him by inches.

It was the first time he had ever been shot at. The tissues of his throat clamped suddenly dry and he stumbled in across the threshold, slamming the door so hard that every pane rattled. There was no safety for him here, but yonder was the door to the kitchen. His knees were a little unsteady as he made for it. He blundered against a table in passing, caught the sharp corner painfully on a thigh muscle. Then he was across the dining room and shouldering through the door, and moist heat met him.

The man who had waited table was at the huge black woodburner, stirring the contents of a boiler. At the sink, a woman was draining a pot of boiled potatoes and stood engulfed in clouds of steam. They stared at the intruder; the man shouted something but Wheelock hurried right past, without breaking stride.

There was a rear door and he went through, to emerge amid trash and weeds behind the hotel.

He held up here a moment, to get his bearings. He thought briefly of Sheriff Rankin, somewhere inside, but at once dismissed all thought of help from that quarter, or any other. He had bought himself no more than minutes; already he could hear voices shouting back and forth, yonder in the street, and couldn't doubt that the Flaggs would quickly be pouring through the building looking for him. He needed a place to hide, if he could find one. And he needed a weapon.

Then, peering along the backs of the scattered row of buildings, he saw the livery stable's rear, with its corral and feed troughs. At once he turned and started for it at a run. At the hotel corner he paused long enough to check the street before crossing the open to the next building. Wet weeds whipped at his boots, and then the stable was before him. He slid between a couple of bars of the corral, and made for the black opening of a door.

Inside he moved hastily, hunting through the stalls for his roan. He found it quickly enough; the saddle cinch had been loosened but the rig and his gear were still in place, following the instructions he had given. When he slipped into its stall the roan swung its head and nudged him in friendly greeting; he gave the sleek neck a slap and then fell to work at the fastenings of his saddlebag, with fingers that shook a little. He fumbled it open, lifted the flap and dug out the gun he kept there.

He owned neither holster nor cartridge belt, since there had never been any reason he could see to wear the gun. Quickly, working mostly by feel in the half-darkness, Wheelock rolled the cylinder and checked to make sure it was loaded. There were extra shells, in a nearly empty box; he was searching the bottom of the pouch for them, when he heard the scrape of boot leather in the aisle just beside him.

He whirled toward the sound, startled. In the center aisle Joe Cooley stood frozen, mouth agape as he found a gun's muzzle unexpectedly pointing at him. The hostler tried for speech, croaked hoarsely and swallowed and tried again. 'Don't shoot! Please don't shoot!' He raised both hands, the words tumbling out of him. 'It—it wasn't *me*, mister!'

Burn Wheelock scowled. '*What* wasn't you?'

'*I* never told 'em! I never said a word to the Flaggs—if Mase Flagg says I did, he's a liar! I wasn't listening to you and the sheriff. I never heard anything. Not a single damn word . . .'

With every frantic syllable, of course, the truth came clearer. Wheelock recalled the talk he and Rankin had held there by the street door, with the rain sheeting down outside, and was aghast to think how much the man *had* heard, and how much he could have passed on to Rufe Flagg's kin. No wonder they had started shooting, the moment they laid eyes

69

on him!

Cooley must not have liked what he saw in his face, for the man started protesting his innocence again. 'Will you shut up, damn it?' Wheelock snapped at him. 'I got to think!'

The frightened voice broke off; jaw unhinged, the hostler stood there blinking at him.

And in that moment, listening to him breathing heavily in the musty stillness, Burn Wheelock grew aware of another sound he knew he had been dreading all along to hear— the approaching trample of boots, out beyond the livery's wide-open street entrance. All he could think of was that the Flaggs had found out, somehow, where he'd got to—and even now they were closing in!

CHAPTER SIX

Wheelock stood frozen, gaping helplessly at the door while Joe Cooley whimpered somewhere close at his elbow.

And then, he saw them.

They were the Flaggs, all right; eight of them, by hasty count. He watched in astonishment as they went prowling by, splashing mud and slop—straight past the barn, without so much as a glance in its direction.

70

For a long moment after they had vanished he stood wondering. All at once it hit him. He *knew* what those men were after, and he swore and went lunging from the roan's stall toward the door. Cooley didn't get out of the way fast enough and a blow from Wheelock's shoulder sent him reeling.

The Flaggs weren't particular as to their victims—searching for Burn Wheelock, they had found Harper Youngdahl instead, and seemed perfectly happy to switch targets. Youngdahl and the pair he brought from Y-Bar had dismounted in front of the stage station. Their talk had broken off and they were staring at the approaching Flaggs.

No one on either side seemed to have noticed Wheelock, in the livery-stable entrance. They were all of them too busy listening to a tirade from Noah Flagg.

The old man stood out there in the sun, with the street mud steaming around him and his thin, hating voice calling Harper Youngdahl every foul and vicious name he could ever have heard of. It turned Wheelock numb, just hearing him; and now as the words spewed forth without a break, his audience began to grow—townspeople, moving into the open but staying at the edge of things, well back out of the way. They listened too, as though in a kind of revolted fascination.

Even Noah Flagg had to run down. He broke off finally, and Harper Youngdahl

71

straightened his shoulders and started an answer. After about two words, his voice was drowned in a chorus of jeers and catcalls. When he was able at last to make himself heard, Youngdahl demanded coldly, 'Do you people intend to let me say a word, or not? Noah, I regret terribly what happened to your son. It's not what I'd have wanted for any man, however much he might deserve it.'

'Who says he deserved it?' the old man roared. 'Did any judge sit on his case? Did any jury bring in a verdict? *Murder* was done to him!'

'And by God,' Mase Flagg cried, brandishing a hogleg revolver, 'we're gonna get them that done it!'

If Harper Youngdahl was frightened he gave no sign, though he was clearly unarmed. His voice took on a note of angry scorn. 'The lot of you are drunk! Don't make any mistakes...'

That got him a furious cursing from old Noah Flagg, and in almost the same instant someone fired.

Burn Wheelock never saw which of the Flaggs pulled the trigger. Mud gouted up within inches of Youngdahl's boot. The rancher involuntarily stepped backward; Jess Croy, standing beside him, let out a startled cry and grabbed out the gun from his holster. Mason Flagg saw this and swung his own weapon around at him, firing hastily—too hastily: for Tom Shecky took the bullet meant

72

for Croy. It doubled him up and he fell sideward, stumbling against Croy, throwing the foreman off stride.

With the echoes of the two shots slapping against the building fronts, Wheelock remembered the gun in his own hand and belatedly he brought it up, with no clear notion of using it. At that instant confusion struck the ranks of the Flaggs.

From somewhere, a man had come wading into their midst, roaring with fury and catching the lot of them by surprise. It was Sam Rankin—in shirtsleeves and bareheaded, exactly as he must have rushed from his hotel room on getting warning of what was happening in the street. His ruddy features showed dark anger and he was laying about him with the barrel of a six-gun, using it as though it were a club. He got to Mason Flagg and smashed the taller man a blow that knocked the hat from his head and the smoking gun from his fist, and dropped him to hands and knees. Without breaking stride the sheriff gave a backhand swipe of the weapon to a second man, tumbled him as well. Youngdahl was forgotten then as the Flaggs became aware of danger sweeping through their own ranks. They broke apart, yelling as they tried to give ground before the slashing menace of that gun barrel.

Rankin went right through them, making directly for the leader—and old Noah Flagg,

73

seemingly as fuddled as the rest, simply stood and watched him come. Then, out of the edge of his vision, Burn Wheelock glimpsed one of the Flaggs taking a sideward step to gain room as he brought up the shotgun he'd been holding slackly in one massive fist. Its twin bores had settled full on the sheriff's chest.

With a shout he was sure no one heard, Wheelock rushed forward and caught that man by the shoulder, hauled him around and shoved his revolver into his middle, hard enough to send the breath gusting from him. The shotgun went clattering to the ground and Wheelock set a boot on it.

For a frozen instant his glance met Rankin's. The sheriff was staring at him with an unreadable expression, but it must have been clear that Wheelock had prevented the barrels of that shotgun from being emptied into him. For only that one instant their gaze held. After that Rankin turned back to Noah Flagg, and his voice seemed to shear straight across the hub-bub around them. 'Call it off, old man!' he ordered harshly. 'I won't have this!'

Everything seemed to stop all at once. Caught in a grotesque variety of poses—a couple of them sprawled in the mud and clutching their aching skulls—the Flaggs returned the sheriff's look but nobody spoke, not even Noah Flagg whose face seemed to swell with the congestion of his anger. For some reason he held his tongue and the sheriff

74

turned to consider the three from Y-Bar. The wounded Tom Shecky lay moaning with Harper Youngdahl hovering anxiously beside him. Only Jess Croy had a weapon in his hand, and he seemed to stiffen as he felt the lawman's stare.

'You too,' Rankin told him crisply. 'Put away the gun.'

Croy's thick-shouldered body settled; he made no move to obey, and Wheelock saw the sheriff's head come up as he realized he was being defied. 'You arrogant bastard!' Temper rough-edged his voice. 'I won't tell you again...'

'Jess!' That was Youngdahl. 'Do as you're told!'

Croy whipped his head around. 'Did you hear what he called me?'

'I heard him tell you to holster that thing. Now, do it—before someone else winds up in even worse shape than Tom!'

As though it cost him an effort, Jess Croy let his gun off cock and rammed it savagely into the holster; the black look he gave Sam Rankin was eloquent enough. The sheriff, ignoring him now, was looking at Youngdahl as the latter went down on one knee to examine his hurt puncher. 'How bad is it?'

With spare and deliberate movements Youngdahl got the denim jacket laid back, the bloodied shirt ripped open. 'He's breathing, anyway.'

75

'Good!' The sheriff came around on his heel. 'This crowd,' he told the Flaggs coldly, 'had better hope so!'

Old Noah Flagg found speech. 'Why the hell should we? When he was probably one of them that lynched my son!'

Burn Wheelock saw how the sheriff's face stiffened. The old man saw it too, and the look in his mean, splayed eyes turned meaner than ever. 'You think we didn't know? Hell, we know you got the proof to pin Rufe's lynching on this Y-Bar outfit—but, we ain't seen you make any move to do it!'

The sheriff told him bluntly, 'I never move till I'm ready, and know I have a case. Right now, you ain't making the job any easier. I understand how you feel about your son; just the same, I'm going to ask the lot of you to get on your horses and ride home.'

'You ordering me out of this town?' Noah Flagg roared. 'You ain't got the authority!'

'Authority enough!' the sheriff snapped. 'You're all drunk and disturbing the peace, and you didn't miss far killing a man. The burying you came for is finished; you got no further legitimate business here. So now you're going to turn around and walk back down the street, to where you left your horses. And I'm going to be right behind you!'

Burn Wheelock sucked in his breath, seeing this as some kind of a showdown. If it meant open war—right here on the street, and right

76

now—he knew he was already committed. Even despite his own troubles with Sam Rankin, a deeply ingrained respect for the law determined that if it came to violence between the sheriff and the Flaggs, he would have to back Rankin's play.

But now it looked as though it might not come to that. Noah Flagg's determination seemed to crumble, almost visibly, before the sheriff's steady and implacable stare. The old man swung his shoulders angrily and turned away—to come up against his son Mason. The latter was on his feet again, holding the gun he'd dropped; a fine trickle of blood through beard stubble marked where Rankin's gun barrel had split the skin. He was almost screaming with fury. 'You ain't knuckling under, Pa? There's enough of us to settle with him, and Y-Bar, and the whole damn town if need be!'

Noah Flagg gave him a long look; he shook his head and grunted, in sour disgust, 'Don't be a damn fool. Or don't expect *me* to be—I got responsibilities!' And he deliberately walked around his son and started away down the street.

His authority had its effect, drawing the rest, however reluctantly, after him. Mason Flagg was the last to yield. He threw a last baleful look at the Y-Bar men; let it rest for a moment, chillingly, on Burn Wheelock. After that a prodding word from the sheriff turned him and sent him after his kin, in the direction of Silvertooth's. He stalked away with Sam Rankin following close at his back.

The tension seemed to leak through Wheelock's nerve ends all at once, leaving his knees shaking—he hadn't realized just how tight-strung he really was. He walked on across the street now, toward the place where Harper Youngdahl was making a closer inspection of the hurt puncher. Wheelock hunkered down beside them, elbows on knees, six-shooter dangling by a finger through the trigger guard. He knew nothing of bullet wounds; he asked anxiously, 'Will Tom be all right?'

'I think so,' the rancher told him. 'Seems nothing too much worse than a crease. The bullet could have churned him up, bad. He was lucky.'

'I'm glad.' He meant it. He was sorry to see his friend in this state—soaked in his own blood, eyes glassy with shock and pain. Even though he had let himself be browbeaten into helping Jess Croy with a lynching, Tom Shecky was actually a good enough fellow. On his own hook, he would never have had anything to do with such a business.

Burn Wheelock asked, 'What happens now?'

'Why, I don't want him riding for a day or two. We'll get him into a bed at the hotel, and get him bandaged. He can stay there until he's able to manage the trip back out to the ranch.'

'That's not what I meant, exactly,' Wheelock said, and he indicated the Flaggs. Youngdahl plainly understood; he followed the look, silently frowning. By turning his head Wheelock could see now that some of the townsmen had ventured into the open, but they were holding back as though this trouble might prove to be contagious. They wanted no part of it.

'Something was started here,' Youngdahl said slowly, 'that I can't quite see the end to. I'm really sorry *you've* had to get into it deeper, Wheelock—you being the one man who did his best to try and save Rufe Flagg.'

'And what about yourself?' Wheelock demanded. 'This whole thing was none of your doing. Just because you own the brand, are you really going to let yourself be pinned with the blame?'

The rancher ran a palm across his bearded cheeks, his honest face wreathed with doubt. 'What else is there to do? If I expect loyalty from my men, can I do less than return it?'

'But Jess Croy didn't hang Rufe Flagg for you,' the younger man said bluntly. 'He did it for fun!'

That got a furious oath. Quickly, lifting his head, he saw the foreman had walked up just in time to hear. For the latter's benefit Wheelock added recklessly, 'And I hope he's happy with the results!'

'The hell with you!' Croy's cheeks were

congested with angry blood; his hands, drawn up into fists, showed white across the knuckles. 'If you hadn't gone and let Rankin find out where that damn rope came from—'

'Or if you hadn't thought it was a damned funny joke to use my rope in the first place!' Burn Wheelock retorted. 'As for the sheriff, I haven't told him anything.'

'You will! You ain't tough enough to stand up to it, once he really starts working you over. He's told us he means to get the truth out of you—and don't think your little act of backing him against the Flaggs, just now, is going to make any difference!'

'I didn't expect it to,' Wheelock answered hotly; but then Harper Youngdahl cut in on them both.

'Let it go, Jess!' the rancher said in a discouraged tone. 'How much did *you* help things, making him order you to put up your gun? Now, give me a hand with Tom Shecky—he really needs a doctor, if this town had one; but maybe we can get the materials somewhere to do a proper bandaging job...'

Among the three of them, they succeeded in getting the hurt man onto his feet; with help he should be able to walk as far as the hotel. Croy took one arm, Youngdahl the other. But the rancher hesitated long enough for a final word with Burn Wheelock: 'I'd like to see you put distance between you and this affair, while you can. It would make me feel better to think you

80

were out of it.'

They were gone, then. Wheelock stood and watched the Y-Bar men make their way across the puddled street with the injured puncher between them; and he was wishing it could only be that simple. *Just don't try to leave before I say you can*—the sheriff's warning still rang in his head. *I'll take it as an admission of guilt, and I'll come after you and drag you back!*

But if he stayed, how could he be sure Rankin wouldn't eventually drag the truth out of him, and force him to pin Rufe Flagg's hanging onto Y-Bar? For all his stern intentions, was he strong enough to hold out under the kind of pressure the sheriff was fully capable of putting on him?

Standing there with the warm sun sucking moisture from the muddy street about him, he knew suddenly what he had to do.

*   *   *

Noah Flagg, with his sons and nephews mounted and ready to ride, seemed unable to let this go without a parting shot. He held the reins in a tight fist, so that the animal under him tossed its head and flirted its hoofs uneasily to the reminder of the spade bit in its mouth. His own mouth a down-turned, bitter trap, the old man looked down at Sam Rankin with pure and wall-eyed hatred. 'One thing's clear, anyway,' he said loudly. 'We've learned

81

today how the law stands. We know what kind of justice to expect for my son!'

Sam Rankin returned his look. 'Old man,' he said, 'you're wrong. The law is fair, but it's also impartial. I mean to get to the bottom of this business; but if you get in my way again—or go after revenge on your own hook—next time, I'll hit you with everything I've got. Do you understand me?'

Something changed in the other man's ugly face. A hint of caution narrowed his eyes, tightened the corners of his mouth. 'Thanks for the warning! *Next* time, by God, I'll make sure of my ground before I move. I'll be absolutely certain you won't interfere!' And with that cryptic statement he yanked the reins. His horse half-reared as it spun about, and it was already going into motion when its front hoofs struck the ground. With derisive yells, and many a hard look for the sheriff, his kin strung out behind him.

Sam Rankin had stepped quickly back to avoid being spattered with mud. He stood for long minutes staring after the Flaggs, his ruddy, weather-beaten features whipped by anger. His hands were pulled up into fists; he forced them open and wiped his palms against his trousers.

Abruptly he turned and started back along the street, with an iron purpose and an impatient, reaching stride. When someone hailed him from a doorway he gave no sign of hearing; he halted only when he reached the spot where the confrontation with the Flaggs and Y-Bar had taken place, and found it deserted. As he looked about, scowling, the hostler from the livery barn came sidling toward him.

'Sheriff?' The man was grinning, with the fawning friendliness of a small dog approaching a larger one. 'Would you be looking for that Wheelock fellow?'

'Yes,' snapped Rankin. 'Would you be knowing where he is?'

'He left ... That's right, Sheriff,' Joe Cooley went on hurriedly, as danger kindled in the lawman's stare. 'He just tooken his horse and lit out. I reminded him that you told him he wasn't to leave. All he said was, "To hell with Sam Rankin!" Them was his words.'

Cooley's grin wavered slightly before the steady probe of those curious tawny eyes. He had an impression that Rankin was holding back his temper with tremendous effort. The lawman asked, 'Did you happen to see which way he went?'

'Yes sir. West, down the creek trail...' His informant hesitated. 'One more thing he said, Sheriff—as I come to think of it.'

'Well?'

'He asked, did I know was there a ferry operating at The Dalles, in case a man should want to cross the river. I told him I'd heard there was. So, I guess he must be headed for

Washington State.'

If he expected praise for this cogent deduction, he didn't get it. The sheriff remained darkly brooding; suddenly his mouth hardened and his head came up and he said harshly, 'Fetch me a horse. Quick!'

'You going after him, Mr Rankin?' Cooley exclaimed eagerly—and then thought better of waiting for an answer.

CHAPTER SEVEN

Jess Croy was a good foreman, but of little use in an emergency like this one with Tom Shecky. He did give his boss a hand getting the hurt buckaroo across the street and up to a hotel room, and after that stayed to watch him while Youngdahl went out to get the things he needed from Nate Bowers. But when Youngdahl asked for help in stripping off the bloodsoaked shirt and jacket, Croy was so roughly clumsy about it that Shecky roused from the half consciousness of bullet shock and cried out in pain. Finally Youngdahl had to order his foreman out of the way so he could do the job alone; Croy shrugged and wandered over to the window, where he stood with arms folded as he leaned against the frame and scowled at the street below, apparently indifferent to the injured man's suffering.

84

Youngdahl had brought cloth for bandaging and—Bowers lacking anything better in the way of antiseptic—a bottle of whiskey. He worked with these crude materials, drawing a groan from Shecky when fiery alcohol hit the bullet-torn tissues. There was a sheen of sweat on the rancher's own face as he finished, and got his man stretched out in the bed with the blankets drawn up against the danger of taking a chill. Tom Shecky appeared to be exhausted, and the quantity of whiskey he'd drunk in fortification against the ordeal had begun to have effect; Youngdahl stood a moment looking at him, and afterward walked over to the washstand and filled the basin and set about cleaning up.

'It could be a lot worse,' he pronounced, answering the question Croy hadn't asked. 'Pure luck, I guess.' Using the towel, he saw Jess Croy start to pick up the whiskey bottle. He took it out of his foreman's hand and placed it beyond his reach, saying, 'You don't need any of that! Let's have an understanding, and have it clear! Even you must see now the mess you've made. I told you before—since you did it as my foreman I have to back you. But I don't have to like it!

'There's no question,' he went on, 'but what you'll be Sam Rankin's main target, until such time as he decides to close the books on what happened yesterday. Sooner or later, we can hope he'll have to let it go—at least, if he

85

doesn't turn up anything more than he was able to get out of us. But until then we have to watch our step.'

He could feel the weight of Jess Croy's stare, its anxiety only thinly veiled. 'So what do you think?' Croy demanded roughly, nervously watching the Y-Bar owner.

Letting him wait and chew nervously at his sooty mustache, Youngdahl deliberately finished using the towel. He tossed it down beside the china washbowl, that held the pinkish stain of Tom Shecky's blood, and he said, 'I've been studying on this. Looks to me it's best if you disappear for a while, so I think I'll send you on a little trip to the Upper Deschutes country. I'd been half planning to go, myself.

'After the winter kill we had, this range is carrying only about half as many head of beef as it's able to. Gives us a chance to expand our operation—that is, if we can find anyone with stock to sell. Maybe those Upper Deschutes River outfits; I understand some of them weren't too hard hit. I want you to look into it.'

'When do I leave?'

'Sooner the better.' Rolling down his shirtsleeves, Youngdahl reached for the coat he'd hung on the foot of the bed. 'You get down there, scout around and see how things look. Should you find anything available at a decent price, go ahead and arrange delivery; or, we can send a crew of our own—whatever's feasible. You got a free hand.'

'I guess I know what to do,' the foreman answered curtly.

'But understand, I don't want you gone more than a couple of weeks at the outside. That ought to be time enough for this business over Rufe Flagg to die down; and we're just too damn busy to spare you longer.'

'All right.' Croy straightened from his lean against the wall, tugged his hatbrim lower. 'I better get out to the ranch, then—get my trail horse and put a pack together.' To Youngdahl, watching him start for the door, he seemed suddenly eager to be on his way but trying not to show it.

'You do that,' his boss said. 'I'll be in town tonight, keeping an eye on Tom. Whatever you do, see that you stay clear of Rankin. That may not be too big a problem, though,' he added. 'I understand he's left town.'

Hand on doorknob, Croy paused. 'How do you know?'

'Nate Bowers told me. Bowers is an old woman but not much around here escapes him. He told me he saw Rankin take off in a hurry, down the canyon trail.'

The hard brown eyes narrowed. 'What does that mean, you reckon?'

'I don't know—and it bothers me,' Youngdahl admitted. 'That Wheelock youngster doesn't seem to be around, either. Could be, Rankin's taken out after him—and

87

if that's it I purely dislike to think of him being hounded by the law on our account. The young fellow's been put through enough.'

Jess Croy snorted. 'The hell with him!'

'You're the last one should say that,' Youngdahl reminded him tartly. 'You *owe* Burn Wheelock! Except for him holding his tongue with the sheriff you could be on your way to jail now, on a charge of murder. Had you thought of that? Well, Rankin knows it— and you'd do well not to forget!'

His accusing stare pinned the other man, but Croy had no answer. The foreman's mouth pulled down hard beneath the ratty-looking mustache. His eyes shuttled away from his boss's look, and turning abruptly he wrenched the door wide.

Harper Youngdahl stood where he was a moment, frowning at the closed door and listening to the heavy tramp of boots down the corridor. When they faded, he picked up the whiskey bottle, had a long swig and rammed the cork home with the heel of a palm. He placed a chair next to the bed, then, and set himself to his vigil beside the wounded buckaroo.

*　　　*　　　*

Following the trail downcanyon, Burn Wheelock was bitterly certain in his own mind that Sam Rankin would soon be after him—

was probably already back there somewhere. He had never doubted the hostler would give Rankin a full account of his leaving; he would only trust that the man would be thorough about it and report everything, not omitting the fugitive's questions about a ferry at The Dalles. As he pushed westward now, alongside the rain-swollen creek, he felt the pressure of pursuit and hoped he wasn't cutting his margins too fine.

He'd supposed he was using his head, but now that it was too late he began to wonder about his own cleverness. Would Rankin actually rise to the bait he'd left?

Antelope Creek flowed easily among low rounded hills, under a sky of dazzling blue depths and breaking cloud; with wet rock steaming and shining all about him, Wheelock had to pull his hat-brim low and squint against such brightness. He'd never before ridden this route, over which he understood stock was occasionally driven to the Warm Springs Reservation. About thirteen miles west of town it was supposed to meet a stage road running south from The Dalles—only, Wheelock had no intention of following the creek trail that far.

Presently a turn in the canyon revealed as good a place as any for leaving it, by way of a shallow draw above the opposite creekbank. It was partially masked by a few junipers and other scrub, and looked easy enough to

89

negotiate; satisfied, Burn Wheelock swung his bridles. The roan picked a way over the shingle, pushed through a fringe of willows and stepped daintily into the creek where rounded stones clattered under its hoofs. A swift and shallow current broke around the animal's legs as it crossed over.

When they came out on the canyon's southern rim, the wind was suddenly against them, plucking at Wheelock's hat-brim so that he had to reach quickly to keep it from being snatched from his head. Wheelock pulled it. Other than the blowing of his horse, and the whipping of the wind through bunch grass and dry brush, there was nothing up here to break the stillness.

Somewhere south—perhaps fifty miles across this rock-ribbed and canyon-slashed rangeland, and beyond the barrier of the Ochocos—he ought to find the Crooked River country and the town of Prineville. Surely there ought to be buckarooing jobs to be had, down in that direction; and he would be out of Wasco County, out of the hornet's nest he'd just escaped from.

He lifted the reins, but then let them fall slack again so that the roan, uncertain as to what he wanted, pawed the ground and shook its head as though urging him to make up his mind. Wheelock did, suddenly; he knew he couldn't travel comfortably, not knowing what was behind his back. He dismounted, led the

90

roan into some juniper where he tethered it, and then picked himself a place behind a thick clump of buckbrush, from which to observe the shallow canyon—the crisp and sparkle of the rushing creek, the alternate flow of cloud shadow and sun dazzle caught in that shallow crease in the land. He took off his hat and laid it on the rock beside him, and settled himself to wait.

Time dragged, became a dull monotony. A lizard appeared as if by magic to sun itself, quite motionless, on a flat lava rock surface not two feet from where he crouched; then some slight move he made, to ease a muscle cramp, sent it whisking soundlessly away. Burn Wheelock slanted a look at the sun, and wondered if he had guessed entirely wrong— maybe Sam Rankin attached far less importance to him than it had flattered him to suppose. Wheelock got out tobacco and papers and rolled a smoke, taking great care with it, simply giving his hands something to do. He snapped a match and got the cigarette going, telling himself, *All right! If he doesn't show by the time I finish this...*

He took his time, holding the cigarette between thumb and forefinger—not drawing deeply but letting it burn evenly, doing nothing to hurry the process. It had got down about halfway when, across the stillness, he heard the first distinct sounds of an iron shoe hitting stone.

91

Though it was what he had been listening for, tense nerves leaped. He forced himself to take a last deliberate drag at the cigarette, let the smoke escape from his nostrils in a slow stream as he pinched out the butt and dropped it between his boots. Then, shifting slightly, Burn Wheelock brought out the six-shooter from its place behind his belt and held it on his knee. He found his hand was shaking slightly, and the breath lay shallow in his chest.

Below him, the rider appeared to be coming on at a steady gait. Wheelock listened to the hoofsound swell and fade and swell again, spattering off the sounding board of the canyon walls; he pulled back the hammer of the six-gun, even as he asked himself—could he actually use it against a law officer? The question troubled him. He scowled and said aloud suddenly, 'Well, I ain't going back! I don't care what he does—now that I'm out of it, I won't get mixed up in that business again!'

Then the horseman was in sight, foreshortened from this angle as he followed the bends in the trail; and it was Sam Rankin.

The sheriff rode a tough-looking brown horse, presumably a rented animal from the livery stable. Unmoving, Wheelock sucked in his breath and held it as he watched Rankin approach the point where he himself had quit the trail—this would be the test, the moment that counted. The shallow canyon was floored here with rock, and thinly soiled; he dared to hope he hadn't left any easy tracks, but a lot depended on how sharp-eyed his pursuer was at reading sign.

He had no way of knowing Rankin's abilities; in his uncertainty he half-rose to a crouch and the gun in his hand lifted. And, down below, the rider went straight on without so much as a pause or a turn of the head.

Burn Wheelock stayed as he was until Rankin passed from sight; only after that did he let the revolver off cock, suddenly shaky as the tension leaked out of him. Either he had thrown Rankin off, or the sheriff wasn't looking for him at all. But he couldn't believe that—there was just no other explanation that would put Sam Rankin on this obscure trail along Antelope Creek, at this particular moment.

But granting he might have gained himself some time, he would be foolish to waste any more of it. There was urgency in Wheelock now as he put the gun away and, easing out of his cramped position, returned to where he had left his horse. He secured the reins, checked the cinch, and lifted to the saddle. The roan was rested and eager to travel. 'All right, boy,' Burn Wheelock told him. 'Looks like you get your next feed of oats in Prineville. Let's go find it!'

And he pointed the animal south.

*   *   *

93

Sheriff Sam Rankin had his share of skills, but the ability to read trail sign was not one of the strong ones—he lacked patience and the temperament to concentrate on small details. Once on the track of a man, he stuck to it like a bulldog; he was more inclined to form his decisions, however, on a shrewd, intuitive judgment of what any fugitive could be expected to do. This time he was a good distance west of Antelope before he began to suspect he had misjudged Burn Wheelock— somewhere along the canyon, he'd let himself be thrown completely off.

He reined in to consider, his narrow fanatic's face darkened with a scowl. Softened by recent rain, the soil here in the canyon bottom really should have shown some prints—unless Wheelock had been cagy enough to ride the rocky shingle or even the creek bottom, itself. More likely, he'd climbed out of the canyon at some point and Rankin, suspecting nothing, had missed it. He swore to himself, the lines deep about his bitter mouth.

He had miscalled the turn, that time. He had figured Wheelock as one who might try a trick, but this was one he had not counted on.

Well, there was no good wasting time trying to hunt for sign he might have passed up, nor would he turn around and ride back to Antelope—not just yet. Already he had other plans. He touched up the iron-jawed livery mount with the spur, and sent it ahead.

A few miles farther on this canyon gentled out and debouched into Trout Creek basin, which was cattle range crossed by a toll road leading southward from The Dalles to Prineville. The road spilled down off a plateau and into the basin through the dramatic and rugged gash of Cow Canyon; there was a toll gate halfway down the canyon and, at its foot, a cluster of log buildings that put up travelers and handled stagecoach teams and served meals to stageline passengers. Rankin was still a little distance from the station now, when a mud wagon came rolling out of Cow Canyon behind a four-horse hitch, people crammed inside and on the roof, sunlight smearing off the turning wheels. It passed the sheriff, plastering him with dust, and drew up before the buildings; the passengers alighted, while a man came out of a barn to unhook the team animals and lead them away.

The sheriff took his own time, and everyone from the stage had already vanished inside the station before he reined in and dismounted. A liver-colored hound came wagging up to greet him, but Rankin had no time to waste on animals. He passed this one up without a look, and left it wagging its tail a little slower and looking after him in disappointment. Crossing hard-packed mud to the station doorway, Rankin entered.

It was early for supper, but stage travelers learned to eat anything—anytime it was

95

available. The half-dozen passengers were already seated at a single trestle table, filling their plates as fast as steaming dishes of meat and potatoes and corn bread and beans could be set out by the station agent's wife and hired girl. But Rankin passed up the food. At a pine plank counter across the room, the stage driver—a spare, unshaven towhead named Hennessy—was leaning talking to the proprietor and working at a tin cup full of coffee that had been laced with whiskey. He greeted Rankin with a startled nod.

'Hey, Sheriff! I kind of thought that might be you we passed. But I thought you was at The Dalles. I won't ask if you're here on business— with you, it's always business.'

The stationkeeper invited Rankin to food, or a shot at the bottle; he turned down both offers briefly. Instead he had a question and he put it without preamble: 'Either of you seen a rider, sometime in the past hour? A young fellow—a buckaroo, on a blue roan wearing a Star brand...'

'Ain't been by here,' the stationman said emphatically. Rankin looked at the driver.

'On the road, maybe? Headed north?'

Hennessy denied it, and the sheriff nodded to himself. It was exactly what he had expected. He had never believed for a moment that Wheelock's questions to the stable hostler had been anything but window dressing, asked in the hope of throwing Sam Rankin on a false

96

scent. Moreover, it was his opinion that a man employing such a ruse could be counted on to work by opposites: Having laid the clue that he meant to ride north, he was almost certain to travel instead in the opposite direction.

Rankin's decision was quickly made. 'You got paper and an envelope?' he asked the proprietor brusquely. 'I need to write a letter.' With the cheap tablet and stub of pencil the man handed him, Rankin turned his back on the pair, using the counter for a desk while he wrote his message:

Dear Jim:

You will oblige by watching out for a man believed to be headed toward Prineville. Name: Burn Wheelock. Age, early 20s. Dark complected, 5 foot 8 or 9. Last seen riding a blue roan horse with a Star brand.

This man is wanted as a material witness in a murder case. If he should come to your attention, see he does not get away even if you have to put him under arrest to detain him. And please notify the undersigned at once.

Yrs. etc.
Saml Rankin
Sheriff, Wasco Co.

His message scowlingly committed to paper, Rankin folded and sealed it in the envelope the station owner found for him. On the envelope

97

he wrote, *James Blake, Sheriff, Crook County, Ore.* Looking around for Hennessy, he found the driver had already gone out to supervise backing new teams into the traces. Rankin followed.

'You know the new sheriff at Prineville? Man named Blake?' At the other's nod, he handed over the envelope. 'See he gets this directly. It's official business, and urgent.' Hennessy squinted at the writing on the envelope, which he had already managed to smear with a sweating thumb. He nodded shortly and stuffed it into a pocket of his shirt.

Having no further business here, Sam Rankin went to his horse, got the reins and swung up for the ride back to Antelope.

CHAPTER EIGHT

In two grueling days, Burn Wheelock had seen more up-and-down country than he would have believed. He came to wonder if his idea of cutting cross country, to throw pursuit, had really been all that clever. This was volcanic country, roughing up all the more as he rode south toward the barricade of the Ochocos; he found himself surrounded by a region of weathered lavas and cinder buttes, of tight stream valleys, and of one awe-inspiring canyon along which he followed for a considerable distance.

From its rim he looked down into depths where the few cattle he saw grazing looked about the size of mice. A man felt like a speck, against those distances. A couple of times, across the rocky hills, he had glimpses of riders working the range, but they were miles away and didn't come near him. Once, he caught the lift of chimney smoke from a log ranch house tucked into a cove of rock and timber, and he carefully rode around it.

Such travel was tough on the roan, and it was slow; he had hoped to make far better time, after leaving Antelope and its dangers behind him. Still, the emptiness and solitude and silence made it easy to forget there were other men in the world. Even the hanging of Rufe Flagg began to seem a thing that had happened a long time ago and somewhere far from here. Burn Wheelock's anxiety over putting all that behind him, and with it the chance of being followed, presently lost much of its edge.

Late on the second day, he came down a flinty ridge and discovered the twin ribbons of a wagon road. It held promise of an easier crossing of the timbered hills piling up just ahead. It meant the worst could be over. Tomorrow he would tackle the Ochocos themselves; tomorrow night, or the next perhaps, should find him putting his feet under a table in a Prineville restaurant, and the roan munching decent oats again in a livery stall.

For tonight, trail rations would have to do. Earlier that afternoon he had knocked over a rabbit, the echoes of his shot bouncing away in throbbing echoes that faded against the lava faces; now, having climbed the road into the first lifts of timber, he made his camp in a pine clearing, offsaddled and picketed the roan in a good patch of grass near a spring runoff. He built his fire and, having skinned and cut up the rabbit with his case knife, spitted the pieces on twigs, Indian fashion, and propped them over his fire to broil.

The aroma that came from them, mingled with that of his coffeepot and the scent of burning pine bark, was mouth watering to a hungry man. He settled down, his back to a boulder and his stomach rumbling pleasantly as he watched the sky turn to steel beyond the treetops, and waited for his supper to cook. For almost the first moment since he saw Rufe Flagg dangling lifeless with a rope around his neck, Burn Wheelock began to feel himself at peace with the world.

Yonder the roan left off feeding and lifted its head to gaze in his direction, one eyeball catching a shining glint from the firelight. At another moment Wheelock might have taken warning from that, but just now he was in too relaxed a mood. He leaned forward to feed another stick into the fire, causing the flames to leap and stir and a stream of sparks to spiral upward. If a stick snapped, somewhere in the shadows, the crackling of the fire masked it.

So he had no warning. He was starting a leisurely move to his feet, when a voice he recognized all too well as that of Homer Flagg said out of the darkness, 'You best stay right where you are! We got you covered three ways...'

Disbelief shocked through him, and held him motionless while his heart slogged in his chest. It just couldn't be! He'd been so sure he was alone—that no one could have followed him over that fantastic, broken country. A kind of sickness engulfed him, and then a desperate recklessness.

For convenience, he'd laid his six-gun on a fallen log, close to hand. Now he made a lunge for it. It was an awkward try and he misjudged; his hand touched the gun's barrel and knocked it spinning, and to his dismay he felt it slide across the log and drop out of reach, just ahead of his scrabbling fingers. Sprawled there like that, he stiffened as a gun sounded shockingly near, and a bullet drove into the log and showered him with splinters.

'By Gawd, mister!' Homer Flagg exclaimed into the echoes of the shot. 'You don't listen very good, do you?'

Sick at heart, Wheelock made no attempt to move or look around as he heard them coming at him. Boots tramped the ground and halted somewhere just behind him; he could hear the

101

sound of breathing. Then a hand seized his clothing and Burn Wheelock was yanked to his feet, spun, and flung back against the boulder where he had been sitting a moment ago. He had lost his hat. He peered through a screen of tangled hair as he stood, panting, with shoulders hunched and hopeless defiance in the look he gave his captors.

They were three of the younger Flaggs— Homer, Mason, and one whose name he didn't know. He had an eerie feeling he was looking at duplications of one face and body, with only slight variations. Homer, big and heavy-shouldered, had a hand that seemed to engulf the revolver he held aimed at Wheelock's middle, while Mason was slighter but with a crafty hint of intelligence in his pale eyes. Still, anyone looking at the knobby faces, and the slanting cheekbones, could have seen they were close kin.

Homer's beard glinted faintly reddish in the glow of the fire; his teeth showed as he grinned at the prisoner. 'You ought to see your face, boy! I bet you thought you was all alone. Never expected *us* to walk in on you...'

Burn Wheelock found his voice. He said heavily, 'It's a fact. I never.'

'You shook the sheriff,' Mase Flagg told him, 'but us Flaggs ain't that easy fooled!'

The third, youngest one had just discovered Wheelock's cooking. 'Hey! Would you looka here!' he exclaimed gleefully. 'If he ain't even

102

got grub waiting for us!' He knelt to snatch up the spitted chunks of meat, tossing a couple to his brothers and then settling back on his heels to start gnawing on one himself. Ignoring the fact the rabbit wasn't completely done they all fell to, washing it down with swigs directly from the spout of the coffeepot.

It didn't seem to occur to anyone to offer Wheelock some of his own food, and he didn't ask. The gnawing fear in his belly had taken the place of hunger.

Homer kept up his conversation with the prisoner as he ate. 'No,' he said, obviously enjoying himself, 'that sheriff figures he's tough but he don't know about followin' no trail. He rode right past the place where you clumb out of the canyon, that day. We come along after, and *we* seen it plain as daylight. 'Course,' he admitted, 'it ain't been all that easy, reading sign in the chopped-up country you been leading us across.'

'Happens we know that country, better than most,' Mason Flagg put in between swallows, his jaws working greasily. 'We thought pretty sure you was heading for Prineville, but till you hit the wagon road we couldn't be sure. Had to be careful you didn't try to pull more tricks. Lost time that way.'

Wheelock didn't try to answer. Sick at heart he stood against the boulder and watched them eat, while the sky grew darker and a stiffening night wind rocked the pines. The Flaggs' three

103

horses had been led up and, still saddled, were cropping at the grass under the trees.

Mason Flagg said finally, 'Well, how about let's get down to business!'

'All right.' Homer tossed aside the bone he had been picking at and wiped his hands on his jeans. He took a final drag at the coffeepot, spat out the grounds between his teeth; then all three brothers were on their feet and Wheelock straightened up a little, quickly wary and apprehensive. Homer said heavily, 'You know what we want from you, I guess.'

He had to clear his throat before he could answer. 'Suppose you tell me.'

'I'll tell you, all right! We want *names*. Every name of every Y-Bar man that was on hand, the day you hanged Rufe. Or, you gonna keep on trying to pretend you wasn't there, yourself?'

'Would it do any good if I did?'

'No damn bit of good, Wheelock!' Mason Flagg broke in harshly. 'We've learned a hell of a lot we didn't know, the first time we let you lie to us. We know now it was *your* rope we took from around Rufe's neck. All we *don't* know, is just who it was put it there.'

'Lemme explain it to you,' Homer went on, when the prisoner merely returned their stares without answering. 'Us Flaggs ain't ever going to let up, till them that killed Rufe is settled with. Only, we got that sonofabitch of a sheriff interfering—and though he ain't likely to do

104

anything to satisfy us, he's made all kinds of big threats if we set out to handle matters our own selves.

'Hell! All we want is to punish them that's guilty—but in case Sam Rankin tries to make trouble afterward, we got to be able to say we just done what the law should of and didn't. So, Pa says we have to have the names, and he sent us after you to get 'em—one way or another. It's entirely up to you *which* way, Wheelock!'

Looking into those cruel eyes, Burn Wheelock understood there was no further use in pretending; these men would no longer be put off by claims of ignorance. Facing them, he braced himself for the hard time he knew was coming. He said heavily, 'If I wouldn't tell Rankin, why should I tell you?'

'We can show you a reason or two, I guess,' Homer Flagg assured him. And then he spoke a sharp command to his brothers: 'Mase! Chet!'

They knew what he wanted; they stepped in and before Wheelock could move to prevent it they had him bracketed between them, each seizing the prisoner by an arm. And as they held him like that, Homer cocked a heavy fist and drove it at his face.

He tried to give with the blow but it struck him solidly on the left cheek and ear. Pain exploded and through the roaring in his head he heard Homer's voice saying, '*Now* how

105

about it? Maybe I can jog your memory a little: That foreman of Youngdahl's—that Jess Croy. He was part of it, wasn't he? It was him give the orders—ain't that so? Or, maybe you need more persuadin' ...'

The bruising fists struck him in the chest, the belly. The wind was driven from his lungs and he doubled over, held up only by the hands that gripped him. Another blow jarred his head; he tasted the warm, iron tang of blood.

'Enough?' His tormentor's voice seemed to come from a considerable distance. 'Listen to me, Wheelock! You know you're a damn fool to take a beating, when you don't have to. Tell us what we want, and we'll let you alone—you got our word on it. We're even willing to forget your part in what happened to Rufe. But, keep on like you are and I'll cut you to pieces. And why go through that, for some bastard like Jess Croy?'

It was a good question. Hanging there between Chet and Mason, he asked himself what purpose he thought he was serving, taking such punishment. He knew Sheriff Rankin would say he was a fool, clinging to ideas of loyalty to a brand he no longer even rode for; besides, if he could take these men at their word, they wanted only the ones who actually put the rope around Rufe Flagg's neck. That would mean there was no longer any need to protect Harper Youngdahl; and he certainly didn't owe Jess Croy anything!

106

But what of Tom Shecky, and Owen Davis?

That stopped him. The Flaggs knew there had to have been at least a couple more involved in the hanging party; but how could Burn Wheelock ever feel anything but a traitor, letting himself be forced to name a pair of ordinary buckaroos who were as little to blame as himself for what happened, that day?

He could only stare at his tormentors through a haze of pain; and apparently these men thought he was merely being stubborn, for Mason Flagg said, 'I dunno. Looks like we might have to burn him a little.'

'That, or use a knife,' Homer agreed. 'But, by God! I promise we'll get it out of him—one way or another! We ain't going back to Pa, with nothin' to show for our trouble...'

Burn Wheelock stirred a little. He managed to speak, and blood came with the mumbled words: 'I have to think ... Will you let me sit a minute?'

At an order from Homer Flagg, he felt himself lowered onto the windfall log and there they left him—both arms numbly clamped about his aching middle, the fire warm against his bruised face. Someone shoved fresh wood in and the flames leaped and crackled. Dimly, Wheelock was aware that a bottle had been produced and was being passed around. He heard laughter. These brutes were really enjoying themselves, he thought grimly.

His head sank farther onto his chest.

Ignored by his captors, he toppled slowly sideward and lay that way a moment, eyes closed. Presently he stirred, made a movement as though trying to sit up again—and, without a sound, rolled off the log to the hard ground behind it.

All at once somebody let out a shout: 'Hey! *What the hell—!*'

Prone on his belly, Burn Wheelock was frantically feeling about for the gun he knew had to be here somewhere. He shifted position slightly, then, and felt the hardness of it against his ribs; he rolled, got ahold of the weapon, worked the trigger as he brought it up.

There was no real chance to aim or hope to do more than throw his enemies off for an instant. He fired twice, blindly, and with the flash of muzzle flame smearing his vision he was rolling again, trying to get out of the firelight. He brought up against a pine, and instantly scrambled to circle it and put it between him and his enemies. Still hurting badly, he knelt with his forehead against the rough bark, and felt the night spin slowly around him. A sweaty palm clutched the six-gun, as he tried to remember he'd now used two of the four bullets left after killing the rabbit.

'Sonofabitch!' That was Homer Flagg, raging. 'Did you see? He was playin' possum on us! *Where the hell did he get a gun?*'

Mase, the smart one, pointed out: 'Well, he

ain't got a horse. But he can lose us on foot if we don't stop him.'

Homer shouted an order: 'Chet! You watch the animals.' And with that the other pair were coming at a run.

Wheelock pawed his way up the trunk and leaned there a moment shaking in a way that told him he couldn't hope to stand and fight. In this dense growth, darkness was almost complete even though some grainy remnants of dusk still lightened the sky overhead. Just to his right was a dense clump of brush. He reached it somehow and sank to his knees— barely in time; for here were Mase and Homer, breathing heavily in rhythm with the thud of their boots as they approached at a dogtrot. He could hear spurts of talking—first, Mason: 'We best keep close, so we don't lose touch and start shooting each other.'

Homer answered gruffly, 'Just don't get in front of my gun! He won't be no problem to run down, not the shape I left him in.'

'I ain't so sure. He's tricky. He could still be playin' possum.'

'Like hell!' the bigger one snorted scornfully. 'I tell you, I *hurt* him!'

One all but stumbled into the bush that shielded Wheelock; he swore and his elbow rattled its dry branches and the fugitive made himself small, convulsively drawing up his shoulders. But then he was alone, and he let the trapped breath run thinly through his teeth.

After that, knowing he might have only moments before his pursuers realized they'd somehow missed him, with an effort he forced himself to his feet.

He had enough presence of mind to know he must keep the dazzle of the fire between him and Chet Flagg, left on guard. He used the spot of brightness as the hub of a wheel and circled wide around it, free hand pressed to his belly that seemed to contain live coals where Homer's fists had slugged him; he kept low, letting a screen of pine trunks pass between him and the light like straight black bars. In order to gain the place where the horses grazed, he had to make almost a three-quarter circle, and his nerves tightened with each step as he thought of the time all this was taking.

The horses were in front of him, suddenly— the tough-looking animals belonging to the Flaggs standing under saddle, Burn Wheelock's blue roan with its gear piled atop a boulder and the leather hobbles on its forelegs. He groaned and shook his head, in near despair. Was there anything else he could possibly have done to add to his handicaps?

Taut nerves leaped as a gunshot crashed, somewhere off in the timber. Wheelock's head jerked up, and it was then that he saw Chet Flagg profiled against the fire, peering off in the direction of the shot. He saw the shine of a rifle barrel, and his own mouth went dry. Swallowing, he tried to make his voice tough and full of menace as he called sharply, 'Drop the rifle—and don't turn around! I'm taking my horse...'

That was as much as he got out; with almost the first word, the other man was doing precisely what he'd been warned against. He came about with amazing quickness, the rifle gleaming as he looked for Wheelock. And he must have caught some glimpse, for when he fired it was almost point blank.

Wheelock recoiled from the blast, dimly aware then that the bullet had missed and he was still on his feet. It was sheer muscular reaction that cramped the trigger of his own gun. Chet Flagg was lifted full into the air and seemed almost to hang there for an instant. Then he was down—on his back, the rifle spinning out of his hands; he lay in a limp sprawl with the cherry glow of firelight on him.

He was a young fellow, surely no older than Burn Wheelock himself. And he was the first man Wheelock had ever killed.

Unable for the moment to do more than stand frozen, staring with eyes half-blinded by after images of gunfire, Wheelock was jarred loose as he became aware of voices shouting through the trees. The dead man's kin were returning, fast—he had a moment to tell himself bleakly, *Maybe they wouldn't have killed me over Rufe, but this is a new ball game!* And the thought pulled him into motion.

With but one bullet left in his gun, he had no

choice but to get out of there fast. He turned for a last, helpless look at the roan. Because of the hobbles, he would have to give it up. That left him nothing but one of the ratty, tough-jawed, spur-scarred broncs belonging to the Flaggs. He chose the closest; it tried to dodge from his hand but he caught the reins, and vaulted onto its back. Yonder there was a glimpse of Homer Flagg just coming into the edge of the firelight, gaunt legs working, six-shooter lifted.

Burn Wheelock didn't hesitate. He yanked the horse's head around, pointing it in the direction of the wagon trace, and kicked it hard. The other horses scattered out of the way as they went pounding away from there in the early darkness.

CHAPTER NINE

The animal Wheelock had got in place of his own blue roan was an iron-jawed brute, worn by cruel usage—from the length of the stirrups he judged it might have been Homer Flagg's mount, a gaunt, shag-maned dun he remembered seeing the big man riding. The saddlehorn's leather, he noticed, had split and been patched with a wrapping of wire. All told, he felt he'd made a most sorry trade.

He knew the Flaggs would be after him, of

112

course, and with only the briefest of starts he couldn't afford to be held to the road. It climbed steadily, solid ranks of timber enclosing it on either hand like a wall to pen him in so that his enemies could easily overtake him. Thus, when the trees to his left fell away abruptly, he seized the chance and turned aside, almost without thinking.

He saw at once that he'd blundered into a spring-fed marsh of some kind. Enough starlight shook down to glint on its surface; standing water splashed high and tough, saw-edged grass whipped around his boots. He felt his horse slip, thought for a moment they would surely both go down. But the animal managed to keep its feet, after a scramble, and then they were on dry ground again with trees waiting to close over them. Burn Wheelock hesitated only a moment, and then went into the pines and tackled the rise beyond.

Almost at once he had to drop from the saddle and lead his horse on the reins, as the climbing got tougher. Finally, under a steep face of bare rock upthrust, he had to halt and give himself and the dun a breather—and, if necessary, make a stand.

He had his six-shooter, with one shell left in the cylinder; all his extra ammunition, along with everything else he owned, had been abandoned at the camp when he took flight. Hopefully he made search of the bedroll tied behind the saddle but found only a couple of

113

sleazy blankets and nothing else at all. He shook his head, with a sour grimace—and now the pulse of hoofbeats began to sound along the road, somewhere below. Wheelock came alert, and moved quickly to the dun's head ready to clamp a hand over its nostrils.

The sounds grew and then, without any break in their rhythm, quickly faded again. When silence settled he knew the Flaggs had gone by, but that didn't mean they wouldn't be back.

He took long enough to adjust the stirrups; after that he mounted again and having picked a way around the rock face that blocked him, went on over the crest and down the slope beyond. His instinct was to put as much distance behind him as possible, but he had sense enough to know it would be foolish to try to travel blind, by night and in country where at any moment the horse could stumble and snap a leg. There would be a moonrise shortly, but Wheelock was in no shape, himself. The beating he'd taken from Homer Flagg was a sickness all through him; in the aftermath of his capture and escape, topped by the killing of Chet, he was having trouble even holding the reins. And the crowbait dun, too, must have covered a lot of miles that day.

They stumbled into a hollow where no one was apt to come at them from more than one direction, and there Burn Wheelock dragged himself out of the saddle. He stripped the

114

horse, and tethered it in such grass as was available. There was nothing at all for the rider to eat, but he didn't really care. Not daring to build a fire, he poked around his chosen campsite with a stick, to roust out possible rattlesnakes. After that he rolled up in Homer Flagg's blankets, trying not to think about the wild life he might have to share them with.

Tired as he was, sleep wouldn't come. Every bruise and sore place was a reminder of what had been done to him; and when he closed his eyes it was to see the horrifying image of Chet Flagg going down, with the firelight on that slack, lifeless face. A second violent death, now—and no clear end in sight, if he wasn't somehow able to lose the Flaggs off his trail.

In pure dread of tomorrow, he found himself futilely wishing he'd never followed his fortunes into this Oregon country.

But in the next breath he began to get mad. Damn it, there was not a friendlier-intentioned fellow in the world than Burn Wheelock, one with less wish to cause anybody harm. In all this grim affair he'd wanted to do nothing but what was right, according to his view of a buckaroo's code of ethics. So, where was the justice? Why should he be hounded, by the law on one side and by that brute clan on the other? It seemed a lot more punishment than he in any way deserved.

On such a note of defiance his thoughts unraveled, and he passed into troubled sleep.

He woke to a gray world without color, morning fog shrouding the ridges and shutting away the sun; for a panicky moment he couldn't remember where he was or what had happened, but sight of the dun horse brought it all back. Wheelock groaned a little as he rolled out of his blankets, shivering in the dank chill.

The dun gave him a suspicious stare in greeting. Now that he had a good look, he could see it was an ugly beast, all right, mean-tempered and stringy muscled; but having any other master than Homer Flagg might have made a difference. The cruel spur marks, and generally gaunted condition, roused Wheelock's pity; he started to lay a sympathetic hand on the bony neck, snatched it back again as the surly animal made a move to snap it off with bare yellow teeth. 'All right, damn you!' he grunted. 'A truce, huh? I traded a hell of a good cow pony for you; since we're stuck with each other we better try to get along.' As he hoisted the beat-up saddle into place and strapped it down, he was thinking regretfully of the blue roan, and all his personal gear he'd never see again.

No supper last night, no breakfast this morning. He thumbed his belt buckle to the next notch and swung astride, wondering how long it would take him to get down out of this fog that seemed fair to shake a man's joints loose. Even an empty stomach could be bearable, with a few rays of sunshine to warm the chill out of his bones—and the stiffness left from yesterday's beating.

The fog moved in wisps and tatters through the heads of fir and larch as he rode on. He kept wondering about the Flaggs—whether they were still hunting for him, or if hopefully they might have given up and turned back. Once, a hint of movement a little to his right caught Wheelock's eye and he twisted sharply in the saddle, dragging out the gun from behind his waist belt.

A buck mule deer drifted out of the trees, its antlered head lifted, and ghosted slowly down the clearing. He was hungry enough that he almost tried a shot, but it was too much distance for a handgun and besides he didn't dare use his only bullet. Better an empty stomach, than an empty gun in an emergency. Regretfully he let the hammer down and put the weapon away.

He climbed higher in the fog and toward midmorning found, with luck, a low pass that was no more than a timbered saddle. Crossing this, he picked up the beginnings of a tumbling creek and a dimly marked game trail that should take him lower. It did, and presently the cloud ceiling began to burn off, the dead gray taking on a blue tinge that steadily deepened. Trees and rocks, and water runneling beside him, took on sparkling color as the sun came warmly through, at last; Burn Wheelock began to be cheered considerably.

117

He rounded a point of rock, then, and a narrow, timber-walled canyon lay below him.

As he pulled in to study it his first thought was that he'd seldom seen prettier or likelier country for raising cattle—the sheltering hills for timber, good haymeadows along the valley bottom, a clear stream affording water for stock or irrigation. In fact, a holding corral built of pine poles showed that someone was, or had been, using the canyon in just that way. And then, looking closer, he made out the ruts of another wagon track, following the near bank of that nameless stream. He eyed them narrowly, and for a moment had to quell the impulse to turn his horse and get away from there.

But nothing moved along the road and he decided he might as well learn the worst, so instead he sent the dun to pick and scramble its way down the last steep drop. Approaching on the level, he discovered that the road's surface was still streaked black with last night's dew; when he got down from his saddle to check for sign, he could see beyond question that no one had used it in several hours.

That meant the Flaggs hadn't come this way ahead of him and he'd be ready to wager they weren't at his back, either. It really looked as though he'd lost them, and for the first time in hours he filled his lungs with a deep and easy breath.

But he wasn't out of trouble yet, as he

118

discovered as soon as he remounted. Now that they were on even ground again, it became quickly obvious the dun was favoring its near front hoof—a thing not noticeable earlier when they were picking a way over rocky footing. He got down again, swearing a little, and persuaded the animal to let him take a look.

The horse had thrown a shoe, at some point up there in the rough going, and its hoof was already starting to split in a way that could spell trouble if it weren't checked. Wheelock shook his head as he looked around, helplessly. There was nothing to be done, at the moment, short of locating a ranch or a homestead where he might find the tools and another iron to replace the one that was lost. For now, he could only mount the saddle again and ride ahead, anxiously watching for signs of habitation as the twistings of the canyon opened new vistas.

As it was, he smelled smoke before he sighted it, rising in a thin gray spiral above a clump of trees; presently the house came into view, the smoke drifting from its chimney. Wheelock's narrow glance was busy as he neared. The house was of unpeeled logs, with a shake roof—likewise, the barn and the few other buildings that made up the place. A pole corral had a couple of horses in it, a ranch wagon stood parked nearby. Certainly this mountain spread appeared well situated, with a wide stretch of meadow behind it and the timbered canyon wall beyond—though he didn't notice any cattle. Wheelock pulled up and considered the layout carefully, deciding whether it looked safe. Anyway, he had no option. If there was a chance here of seeing to his horse's needs, he would have to take it.

A narrow log bridge spanned the creek, the clear water swirling underneath; he crossed, and followed a wagon track that curved up the mud bank and brought him into the yard. Now, on closer inspection, his experienced eye could begin to pick out certain signs of neglect. Roof shakes on the house were badly curled by weather, a number missing entirely. One leaf of the barn door sagged badly on a broken hinge. When he checked the horses in the corral, making doubly certain neither of them looked like one of the Flagg's animals, he saw that the top pole was partly down, aslant from its fastening to a single upright. Small things, but they added up...

A voice said, 'Young man? Were you looking for somebody?'

He turned hastily. The woman had appeared at the door of the house while his attention was elsewhere; she stood on the stoop, peering at him with an arm upraised against the glare of noon-high sun. She wasn't a young woman—in her mid-forties, he would guess. She had a sweet face but it showed lines of anxiety and the dark stains of weariness, like

120

bruises, about her eyes; the fair hair, drawn back into a bun, had gone a trifle dull. She was watching him uncertainly and Burn Wheelock explained quickly: 'Not looking for anybody—no, ma'am. It's my horse; he's flang a shoe. Thought maybe I could get it seen to, here.'

He had thought she might be reassured to know he wasn't looking for a handout, a conclusion she might easily have drawn; but that didn't seem to be the problem. She looked puzzled—as though somehow disappointed, and yet at the same time relieved. He had a sudden feeling that, seeing him, this woman was half expecting news she didn't really want to hear.

When she only looked at him, her continued silence made him a little irritable. 'Look, ma'am. I don't want to be no bother, but I really got to do something about my bronc. Would you have such a thing as a forge, and an anvil?'

'Why—yes,' she said, stirring herself, and he sensed then that her silence hadn't been aloofness but extreme timidity. She made a vague gesture. 'In the barn, there. Only—'

Baffled by such indecisiveness, Wheelock didn't know whether to try and jar her out of it by arguing, or simply proceed to do what was needed without invitation. But perhaps, he thought, he really should go away from here without upsetting her any more than he

121

already had...

For his own urgent reasons, that was simply out of the question. As he debated how to handle the situation, and the dun began to move around restlessly, another woman stepped out through the door to join the first.

She was speaking as she came, saying, 'Mama, is that—?' The timbre of her voice, the quick firmness of her step, marked her at once as someone younger, and when he saw her Wheelock automatically lifted a finger as though to touch his hatbrim—forgetting he'd also left his hat, last night, when he escaped from that camp back in the hills. Then he saw the girl's face and his arm hung there foolishly, the gesture forgotten.

Yes, it was the woman's daughter all right. She too would have looked like that, before her hair lost its young luster and her blue eyes took on their worried cast of anxious middle age. Men must have stared at her the way Burn Wheelock stared at her daughter now, forgetting everything else for the moment in the first unexpected impact.

A pretty girl must have to get used to being eyed like that. Her return look was coolly impersonal; she seemed to lack completely the older woman's timidity. 'Are you from town?'

'No, miss,' he told her. 'Just riding by. Wheelock's the name—Burn Wheelock. I was telling your mother—'

'He says the horse needs a shoe, Rebecca,'

122

the older woman put in quickly. She shook her head, her hands made a helpless gesture. 'Really, I'm sorry. But my husband isn't home just now, and—' Another gesture served to complete the sentence as she let her voice trail off. Her worried eyes appealed to him. It was plain enough that she would like him to leave without being forced to order him, but he didn't see how he could oblige her.

'I do hate to be a bother,' he said again. 'But if I don't do something, he's gonna go lame on me—and he ain't worth an awful lot at best. Shouldn't take me long. I'll leave soon as it's done.'

The girl seemed to reach a decision. 'I'm sure it's all right, Mama,' she said quietly. 'We can't turn someone away who's in trouble. And there's no other place between here and Prineville.'

Her mother lifted her shoulders and let them fall again. 'No—of course, Becky,' she agreed, with a sigh, though her expression was still dubious. Suddenly Wheelock had a picture of himself, reflected in her look, and he knew he didn't look like very much: hatless and unshaven, his face swollen from the battering of Homer Flagg's bruising fists; it all went with the sorry-looking horse and grubby gear. If *he'd* been a woman with a pretty daughter, and no man on the place for protection, he doubted very much if he'd been any more inclined to let him light.

123

Or, had that really been the problem? Somehow he didn't think so. There seemed to be something more . . .

But the girl had made the decision, and her mother said, 'Very well, Mr Wheelock. You should find what you need in the barn.'

'Thank you,' he said politely, trying to sound as respectable as he could. And he reined the dun that way, leaving them standing there and watching him. He had to get down and worry open the door that hung askew, on its rusted and broken hinge; then he took the reins and led the horse inside.

The barn was a mess. Wheelock, who liked his equipment in apple-pie order, looked around and was considerably revolted. Nothing was where it should be. A wheelbarrow lay upside down in the middle of the floor, harness for the wagon team was piled in a tangled heap, there was a murderous-looking rake lying with tines upward. He made a face at the smell of moldy hay; worse, he wondered how long it had been since the stalls had been cleaned.

The smithy occupied one rear corner. There was a forge with a leather bellows, overflowing barrels of scrap iron and plain trash, an assortment of mauls of various sizes lying about . . . and sitting on the anvil, a bottle with a half inch of whiskey in the bottom. Wheelock picked up the bottle and scowled at it a moment, trying to reconcile all this with his

124

impression of the girl and her mother.

Certainly they weren't responsible for the look of the barn; only a man, and a slovenly one at that, could have created this much disorder. But it went further than that. Neither the girl nor her mother seemed really at home in these surroundings. They looked too good. They lacked the weathered, sunburned look of ranch women; and though she wore an apron over it, the older one's dress—he realized now—had been an impractical thing of silk, with trimming on the front, more the kind of thing you would expect her to wear when welcoming visitors into her parlor, for tea.

He shook his head over the matter, placed the bottle in a trash barrel, and stripped out of his jacket.

A working buckaroo could do almost any job that came up, and now Burn Wheelock turned blacksmith. He found enough charcoal to build a fire in the forge, located a handful of shoe blanks in the bottom of an overturned barrel and measured one against the dun's hoof for fit. The split, he decided, was no great damage and needed no treatment. As he scraped the hoof with a drawknife he gave an uneasy glance from time to time toward the door, that allowed a view past the house toward the wagon road; but he never saw a sign of the Flaggs or of anyone else. Once he walked over to the entrance for a better look—and caught sight of the girl standing in the house doorway. He drew back quickly, not wanting her to imagine that he was spying. But as he returned to his work, he felt a faint stirring of interest at the thought she might have been wanting a look at *him*.

Not likely, he told himself, fingering the stubble of beard. Probably her mother had sent her to check and try to find out how long that range tramp meant to fool around in the barn...

Having made certain no other shoes needed replacing, he got his fire hot, working the bellows rope until the iron thrust into the coals glowed red. At the anvil, afterward, strokes of the hammer chased echoes around the dark barn rafters. The dun horse bared its teeth and threatened to rip the shirt off Wheelock's back, but he got the leg gripped firmly between his knees and, by dint of considerable cussing and sweat, got the iron nailed on.

When he was ready to leave he lifted the broken door again and muscled it into place, its bottom edge scraping. He stood a moment with the reins in his hand, looking across at the house and wondering if he ought to stop there and thank Rebecca and her mother again; he decided against it, since they would probably prefer not to be bothered any more than they already had. So he shrugged, and toed the shabby stirrup, and lifted into saddle.

CHAPTER TEN

Riding past the corner of the house, he reined in suddenly.

The girl was there, chopping kindling. She had put on a man's shapeless hat to keep her hair in place, she had rolled up the sleeves of her blouse, and she was making a valiant effort. But the long-handled ax seemed to weigh nearly as much as she did, and she obviously didn't know how to take a grip on it. She had set a length of stovewood on end and the axhead shone in a bright streak as it came down, carried by its own weight. It struck the chunk a glancing blow that merely knocked it over.

She leaned the axhead on the ground, with a sigh of exasperation as she ran her wrist across her forehead. After that she set the chunk of wood upright again, but before she could lift the ax for another try Burn Wheelock was down from his saddle, to take it from her.

Rebecca tried to hold on but he was firm. 'Lady,' he exclaimed, 'that's the way to chop off a foot!'

She let him have the thing, with a little gesture. 'I'm getting better at it than I was,' she insisted.

'A body's bound to improve at anything, with practice. But you don't look big enough to handle this. Anyway, I'd like to repay the courtesy for letting me fix up my horse.'

She didn't argue the matter—a clear sign of a practical sense that he liked. 'It's not at all necessary,' she told him. 'But if you really want to do it, I'll certainly let you.'

'I really do want to.'

The girl backed away and let him take over. Having an audience lent speed to his arm, and determination to make a good showing. The blade flashed, the white pine split apart laying its clean scent on the noontime stillness, the pile of kindling swiftly grew. But after a few minutes the mother's voice sounded, calling the girl's name; Rebecca said apologetically, 'Mama wants me to help her with something. Excuse me.'

The woodpile was low; before he finished and set the ax aside he had chopped up everything in sight. It made a good double armload, under which he staggered slightly as he mounted the back step and gave a kick to the jamb beside the open door. 'Where do you want this?' he called.

The girl appeared. When she saw his armload she exclaimed, 'Oh, my goodness! Right over here—the box by the stove.' She made way for him and he managed to edge inside without dropping anything.

After the brilliant sunshine the kitchen was like a warm, dark cave at first, but he located the gleaming polished trim of the big wood

128

range. The box beside it had been nearly empty; he filled it with a thunderous clatter, and afterward picked up a few loose lengths of kindling that had spilled over. He balanced them on top and, straightening, looked at the bark chips clinging to his clothing. 'I hope I haven't made a mess...'

The words died in his throat.

From the oven, and from steaming pots atop the stove, a battery of smells assailed him, compounded of a vegetable stew and pan biscuits and brewing coffee. Having missed breakfast, and supper the night before, Burn Wheelock took the full force of it and it paralyzed him, unable in that moment to do more than stare at the source of those aromas.

He was jarred out of that as he heard the older woman say, 'Are you hungry, Mr Wheelock?'

Shame heated his face, until he could feel both ears burning. He found his voice but it came out as a stammer: 'Ma'am, I never meant—'

'Of course you didn't,' the girl put in quickly. 'But it's dinnertime, and we've more than enough. You're welcome to share it.'

He knew he should refuse, but he lacked the courage. He said desperately, 'Just so you don't think I'm some kind of a grubliner. I ain't! I'm a top buckaroo. But yesterday, I got jumped by some hardcases and lost my rations and all my gear—even my hat. And my horse!

129

That sad-looking thing out there ain't mine, you know—I had a sweet little blue roan, but I don't rightly imagine I'll ever see him again...'

He decided he was babbling, and abruptly made himself stop. But the women were looking at him with real sympathy in their faces. It was the mother who said, in her quiet manner: 'I'm sorry to hear of your trouble, Mr Wheelock. Any of us can fall on bad times. Becky, pour some warm water and get a towel. Our guest may want to wash up before he eats.'

'Thank you,' Wheelock said humbly.

The tin basin sat at one end of the sink; there was a soapdish and a mirror. The girl poured water, steaming, from the teakettle. He wouldn't take off his shirt in the presence of women, but he did his best by rolling up the sleeves and turning in the collar. At a bunkhouse washbench, a man could splash and snort as he pleased; here, Wheelock self-consciously made as little noise as possible. Afterward, he looked at himself in the mirror and fingered a day-old stubble of beard. Having lost his gear, he had nothing to use on it except the case knife that was serviceable enough for skinning and butchering a rabbit—or cutting a dead man down from the rope that held him swinging—but which he doubted would do anything against whiskers as tough as his.

And then the girl was at his elbow. 'Would you like to use this?' In one palm she offered a long-shanked razor.

'It's my husband's,' the other woman explained. Burn Wheelock took it with a nod, tried the edge with his thumb and found it adequate. He made a lather with the yellow bar soap, and scraped his jaws clean, and after running a comb through his hair was better satisfied. Afterward he insisted on emptying the basin, carrying it out back to dispose of the soapy water.

A thought bothered him, and he stood looking around the yard before he realized just what it was: There was no pump at the kitchen sink, and no sign of a well here in the yard. He wondered how these people got their water, concluded they must have to carry it in buckets from the creek, a good hundred yards from the door.

In an age of windmills, there was no excuse for that. He wondered at the kind of man who would make his women put up with such primitive arrangements.

When he went back inside, Rebecca and her mother both seemed to approve the change in him, and he himself felt less like a saddle tramp and better prepared for the unfamiliar ordeal of sitting down to dinner alone with them.

The table was massive, and like the leather-slung chairs was plainly homemade; the whole place had a half-finished look about it. There was one main room, that apparently served most of the purposes of living, with the kitchen

131

area at one end and a fireplace at the other that was made out of mud-chinked lava rock. Wheelock saw a rack of pipes on the mantel, a shotgun and a rifle in a wooden case. Everything looked decidedly rough, decidedly masculine.

Through an open door he caught a glimpse of a big double bed with a patchwork quilt on it—the nearest thing he noticed to a woman's touch, except for what was placed in front of him. For the mother—now that she had overcome her first reluctance at allowing him to light—had plainly risen to the occasion of entertaining company at her table; she had spread a cloth and set out what he suspected must surely be her best dishes.

His coffee cup looked to hold about one good swallow at a shot, and was so eggshell thin he dreaded to pick it up; the water glasses actually had stems. As she seated herself the woman announced, with touching formality, 'Mr Wheelock, I fear I haven't properly introduced myself or my daughter Rebecca. I'm Mrs Susan Telford.'

'Pleased to meet you,' he murmured, and felt foolish enough since he judged the meeting had taken place the best part of an hour before. Altogether, the meal and the elegant manners of his hostess were a strange contrast, and oddly out of place, set against this crudely furnished ranch house in the heart of the Oregon hills. And that Susan Telford sensed it,

132

too, was revealed in the insecurity that looked at him from her faded eyes, even as she smiled at him across the table.

Rebecca, for her part, had fallen silent from some whim of her own, though he could see her watching him whenever he looked at her. But if the setting was strange the food was excellent, and he took pains to say so. Finally, in an effort to make conversation, he tried asking questions: How far would he have to go yet to reach Prineville? Ten miles, the mother told him, following the wagon trail along the creek—McKay Creek—until, on entering Crooked River Canyon, it joined the main stage road this side of town.

Mention of the stage road gave him pause; it reminded him of the Flaggs who, for all he knew, might even now be in Prineville, having lost his trail but expecting him to show up there sooner or later. He put that thought aside to chew over later, and asked, 'If you'll pardon my saying it, don't this place of yours seem kind of far from things? Somehow, ma'am, you strike me as more the kind who'd want to live right in town.'

She gave him her timid smile. 'As a matter of fact, Mr Wheelock, my daughter and I used to live in Omaha before we moved here.'

'Omaha!' he repeated. 'Don't reckon I ever did see a place *that* big!'

The girl spoke up. 'Prineville, Oregon, doesn't look like an awful lot, by comparison!'

133

'I would imagine—though of course, I ain't even seen Prineville.'

'Where are *you* from, Mr Wheelock?' the mother wanted to know—making polite conversation, he supposed.

'I'm just a farm boy, ma'am—from Indiana. My folks died when I was young and it seemed a good idea to head West—missed Omaha, somehow. I've been moving around quite a few years now—cowboying, mostly. Buckarooin', they call it here in Oregon. Of course,' he added, a little ruefully, 'I haven't got a lot to show for it all—and even less than I had when I made camp last night!'

'You told us some badmen held you up and took everything you owned?' Mrs Telford shook her head in sympathy. 'How dreadful! You're fortunate they didn't kill you!'

He wholeheartedly agreed. 'You're plenty right, there, ma'am!'

'It's a hard country. Back in the spring, when we came here, I really had no idea! Why, do you know that right in Prineville—no more than a few months ago—there was violence and killing? Some men who called themselves "Vigilantes" had control and nobody could do anything to stop them. It just went on and on, until finally the people were able to elect an honest county government; and so—thank goodness—that seems to be all over. But while it was going on, I guess no one's life was safe. They even took two men out and *hanged* them...'

Suddenly Burn Wheelock had stopped eating and was staring at his plate, as he tried to down the sick knot that started to rise in him. Mrs Telford continued chattering on, making conversation that he didn't even hear; but when he raised his head he discovered that the girl was looking squarely at him, with a most puzzled expression. He quickly looked away; but as he picked up his fork and began again mechanically eating, he wondered what she had been able to read in his face.

At last the meal was over and Wheelock got to his feet, awkwardly thanking Susan Telford for her hospitality. She protested. 'It really wasn't anything fancy. My husband's been gone a bit longer than he expected, and we're running just a little short of supplies until he returns.'

'Yes, ma'am. But believe me, it was the tastiest meal I've et in a good long time.' He hesitated, feeling strongly obligated to offer some kind of payment but not knowing quite how to put it. 'Ma'am,' he finally managed, 'I noticed one of the top poles has come loose from the corral—probably happened during the night.' He was willing to bet it had been down a lot longer than that. 'You could lose those horses if it ain't fixed. I'd be more'n pleased to see to it, long as I'm here.'

One fine-boned, gentle hand went up in ladylike protest. 'Oh, no, Mr Wheelock! I wouldn't think of it. You were our guest!'

'Wouldn't take but a few minutes,' he insisted. 'And I just wouldn't feel right, leaving it like that. I'll just fetch a hammer and nails from the barn and have it put to rights in no time.'

The girl settled the matter sensibly. 'Why, that would be very kind of you, Mr Wheelock,' she said, turning from the window where she had been looking into the yard. 'Do you know, I just hadn't noticed that pole?' Which was a fib, Wheelock figured. Probably they had both been worried about it—or else, like so much else around here that was wrong, it had been in that shape so long they took it for granted. 'It's our wagon team in the corral—and if you really think there's danger of them getting out, then it certainly would be a neighborly thing to have it fixed.'

Her mother gave in gracefully. 'Well, then—thank you indeed, Mr Wheelock. I hope you won't be putting yourself to too much trouble.'

'No trouble at all,' he assured her, and went out to do the job.

*   *   *

He had to hunt around through the scatter of junk in the barn before he located a hammer and a bag of nails; he was also pleased to locate a length of rawhide that should be even more useful. The actual repair job was no great

136

matter. Wheelock was astraddle of the fence, with the fallen pole hoisted and the strokes of his hammer echoing off the timbered scarp beyond the creek, when he heard Rebecca speak from below.

'I wondered if there was anything I could do to help.'

'Not a thing.' After a couple more whacks, driving the nail deep into the wood, he added, 'Unless you want to take this hammer. Or, stand aside so I don't drop it on you.'

She reached and he handed it down. Afterward he took the rawhide, that he had hung over the fence handy, and began to wrap tightly the juncture of pole and corner post. The girl stood with her head tilted a little on one side, watching him.

Suddenly she said, '"Burn Wheelock." That's a funny first name you've got.'

'Nice you find it amusing,' he answered stiffly.

'Oh, no,' she insisted. 'I just meant I'd never heard it before.'

'It's short for Burnside. My pa was a big supporter of the Union,' he explained, as he went on working with the rawhide. 'I was born in November of '62, just before the battle of Fredericksburg. Pa always claimed, had I come along a couple of months later when Lincoln changed generals, my name would of been Hooker.'

She considered. 'I think I prefer "Burn".'

'It's a name,' Wheelock said with a shrug. 'I generally answer to it ... There—that ought to hold,' he decided, giving the pole a shake. 'Let that rawhide get rained on and shrink up a couple of times, and it will hold like iron.' He climbed down from the fence, then, and took back the hammer. 'I'll put this where it belongs, and be on my way.'

'That was very kind of you, to fix it.'

Now the moment had come when he had no further reason not to leave, he found himself suddenly reluctant. He looked at the girl standing before him, with the wind plucking at her skirt and at the fair curls that framed her face, and he had a feeling that he had made a friend. The road to Prineville seemed all at once a very lonely one.

'No need to mention it, Miss Telford,' he said gruffly. 'It was nothing at all.'

A stronger gust of wind came down the canyon; she put up a hand to set her hair to rights. 'Now you've got *my* name wrong,' she told him, smiling a little. 'It's Savage—not Telford. That was my mother's name, too, until this spring when she met my stepfather and married him.'

'Was that in Nebraska?' Wheelock asked, and the girl nodded. 'I kind of wondered. I mean, it's none of my business of course; but like I said before, you neither one are what I'd expect to find on a ranch out here in the hills.'

'I know,' Rebecca told him, and her voice

was suddenly tired, with a freight of something very near to despair. 'I grew up in Omaha. Papa worked for the railroad until he was killed—an accident in the yards. That was nearly eight years ago.' She looked away from him, toward a big pine that stood beyond the barn with its needles shining in the sun; Wheelock could see only the soft curve of her cheek, and imagine the troubled expression in her eyes.

'Last April,' she went on—and he sensed this was something she badly needed to talk about, and he just happened to be the one on hand to hear it—'Reub Telford showed up and became interested in Mama. He was a widower and I guess he thought it was time to get married again. He talked about his big ranch in Oregon; he seemed to have money to spend. Mama was so tired, from years of fighting the world all alone, that I think it must have been easy to persuade herself he was everything he said he was...'

'Where *is* your stepfather, Miss Savage?' Wheelock asked quietly.

She shook her head, not looking at him. 'I don't know. He comes and goes as it pleases him—we have no idea where, but we always half expect bad news. When he has money, I don't know where it comes from. But you see what this ranch is, that he boasted about!' She lifted a hand and let it fall. 'Right now there isn't even a head of stock on the place.'

'It has the makings,' Wheelock told her. 'It could be a fine spread. At least, I can see it's got good meadowland, and water.'

'I don't know anything about that,' Rebecca Savage said. 'I never really wanted to come to Oregon, in the first place; but I didn't trust that man and I thought Mama might need me. Now that I'm here I think it's beautiful—different, certainly, from anything I ever knew before.' A movement of her hand indicated the green stretch of meadow, the sheltering timber and brown lava rock that rose above the canyon of McKay Creek. 'I think I could learn to love it, almost. If I wasn't always so frightened...'

Burn Wheelock swallowed. There ought to be something he could say, to reassure her; but he sensed her helplessness, and through her eyes he could see what a bleak situation this could be, for two women alone and far removed from any life they'd ever known. He thought of Rebecca's struggle with the heavy ax; he thought of hauling buckets of water from the creek, of the ten miles that separated them from town—and no telling how great the distance might be to the closest neighbor.

Then, before he could find an answer, she was turning to him again. 'Do you suppose you could do us one more favor?'

'Name it,' he told her promptly.

She was hesitant about doing so. 'It just occurred to me—I mean, since you're headed for Prineville, anyway—maybe you'd be good enough to take Mama and me along with you. I'm afraid neither one of us really knows how to handle that team, or even how to hitch them to the wagon. But we're so low on supplies, it's time we simply *have* to get in to the store and try to arrange for some; because I'm really afraid we can't afford to wait any longer on Reub Telford. Would—would it be too much of an imposition?'

'Sho'!' he told her. 'No trouble at all. You and your mother get ready, and I'll hitch up. Only—' Already turning toward the house, she paused with a questioning look. He indicated the hang of the sun. 'It's getting sort of late. Maybe you folks would rather wait till morning, and plan to get an early start.'

'But—you?'

Burn Wheelock dismissed that with a gesture. 'Don't let it worry you. One day's the same as any other, far as I'm concerned. Why don't you leave it to your mother?' he suggested. 'Whatever she decides is fine with me.'

He returned the hammer and sack of nails to the barn where he had found them, and when he came out again Susan Telford was calling him from the doorway of the house. She appeared delighted at the idea of a visit to town, but he had to explain all over again that he wouldn't at all mind staying over, and making the trip in the morning.

So it was arranged; and Burn Wheelock,

with the waning hours of a summer afternoon ahead of him, had already decided what he meant to do with them. First, he took the ax and rode the dun into the timber, hunting firewood. He found a likely looking blowdown, trimmed off some branches, attached a rope to it, and dragged it down to the house. He got there just as Rebecca was starting for the creek with a bucket in either hand. Quickly he dismounted and took them from her, despite her protests. 'But I do this every day,' she insisted.

'Not today, you don't!' he said grimly. And he filled the buckets and brought them back to the house, gruffly turning aside her stammered thanks.

He left off cutting the firewood when the last sunlight was golden on the canyon rim and gray dusk was pouring out from under the trees. He fed and watered the horses and then Susan Telford was calling him to supper.

It was really rather pathetic, Wheelock thought, to see how excited she appeared over the prospect of a trip to town. She had spread herself on the evening's meal, as well as she could from the dwindling stock of supplies; there was homemade bread, split pea soup and canned tomatoes, and the stew left from dinner. She really chattered brightly through the meal—about her life in Omaha, an amusing incident or two during the trip west to Oregon—but never, he realized afterward, with a mention of her missing husband.

Rebecca was drawn into the talk and time passed pleasantly, until at last he broke things off by getting abruptly to his feet with the announcement that it was later than he'd realized—high time he should be getting out to the barn, if they hoped for an early start for Prineville in the morning.

'You're not spending the night in any barn!' the older woman protested. 'We have a cot that can be set up as soon as these dishes are cleared away.' And as he hesitated: 'Please! It feels safer to have a man in the house, somehow.'

He read the honest appeal in her voice and could not refuse, since it gave him a sudden, sharp intuition of her terror and loneliness in her husband's absence. 'All right,' he said. 'I'll check the animals, and be back.'

The night was bracing and crisp, the stars a bright mesh that stretched from timber-jagged rim to rim above the canyon. Returning from his inspection at the barn, Wheelock stopped a moment to listen to the murmuring of McKay Creek, and gaze at the lamplit windows of the house and around the perimeter of the ranchyard.

He knew there was trouble and unhappiness here—where in this world did you get away from them?—but all he could feel at the moment was the peacefulness of the place. The Flaggs, and Sheriff Sam Rankin, and the murderous Jess Croy all seemed very far away;

so did the lynching of Rufe Flagg, and even the face of the young fellow Burn Wheelock had killed—was it only twenty-four hours ago?

Tomorrow he would leave here, just as he left every other place he had ever been. But something told him this was one he wouldn't easily forget.

He shook his head, and walked on toward the house.

CHAPTER ELEVEN

The cot they prepared for him, out in the main room, was apparently where the girl had been sleeping while her stepfather was home; now she shared the bedroom with her mother. Burn Wheelock, acutely conscious of their presence beyond the closed door, thought he probably would have slept better in the barn. But his bed was comfortable, and he didn't waken until nearly full day. Then, hearing the women's voices as they moved about in the adjoining room, he hastily dressed and got out of there.

He was feeling really good, only a few nagging hints remaining of the beating Homer Flagg gave him. At the barn, he even whistled tunelessly as he started putting together a serviceable set of harness for the wagon team, and waited the call to breakfast.

Mrs Telford looked somehow younger this

144

morning, dressed in what he thought must be her best and flushed with the excitement of a break in the lonely monotony. When, the meal finished, he rose from the table with the purpose of getting the wagon team hitched up, Rebecca followed him outside. 'I want you to show me how it's done,' she explained, 'so I'll know what to do when Mama and I come back later, by ourselves.'

Wheelock saw the point of that, and accordingly he showed her the harness and explained the uses of each strap and buckle. Afterward he got the team from the pen and backed them onto the shaft, one by one, and demonstrated how to snap the tugs to the singletrees. The animals were restless after being left in the corral so long and acted up and moved around and he had to shout at them and haul them into their places; he thought the girl looked a little solemn over the prospect of having to manage these beasts that were so much bigger than herself.

'Just don't take anything off them,' he said. 'They're big—but remember, it's brains that count, and most horses are pretty dumb. Pulling a wagon is just about all these fellows know, and they're only really comfortable when they're doing it.'

She nodded but she didn't seem too certain.

At the risk of speaking out of turn, Wheelock asked her suddenly the question that had been nagging at him: 'Tell me, do you have any idea at all how long this man Telford figured to be away, this time?'

'No,' she admitted, looking not at him but at her hand as she stroked a dusty shoulder of one of the team. 'He's a secretive man, and he tells only what he wants to. He's been gone a lot, since we came here; he never says where—it's always just "on business." But this is the first he's stayed so long. Two weeks tomorrow...'

'And he didn't think it important to leave any money, or enough food to last you?' He added bluntly: 'It makes you wonder how his first wife was able to put up with him.'

'He never told us much about her, either,' Rebecca said. 'Except that she died of pneumonia and he buried her in Prineville. I don't know her name, or how long they were married. Apparently he went through the house and got rid of everything that had belonged to her.' She hesitated. 'But tucked away on a shelf, I found a box that he must have overlooked. There wasn't much in it—a pair of nice gloves, that looked as though she kept them for special occasions; a lace handkerchief, and a Bible. And a baby dress, folded away in tissue paper. I don't think they ever had any children, but maybe she was hoping.' Rebecca shook her head. 'It makes me feel as though I knew the woman—and makes me sad for her.'

Not only for her, Burn Wheelock thought bleakly. *Maybe someday they'll find another*

146

box with your mother's hopes and dreams laid away in mothballs and folded paper! But he didn't say it aloud; and next moment Susan Telford, parasol in hand and ready to leave, called to them from the house. Wheelock had already saddled his horse and tied it behind the wagon; he helped both women to the seat, climbed up beside Rebecca and yelled the team into motion. A moment later they were rolling out of the yard and across the bridge, and onto the rutted road that followed McKay Creek south toward Prineville.

It was going to be a fine day, the sun warm and the wind cool, and the last of the morning mist lifting in tendrils off the sparkling creek surface. It felt odd and yet pleasant, too, to be perched up on a crowded wagon's seat with Rebecca in a pert straw hat decorated with artificial cherries, and her mother holding her parasol as a shield against the sun. Both women seemed to be enjoying a change of scene, despite the hard seat and the slow, jolting travel. Wheelock kept the horses moving but he didn't push them.

Presently Rebecca insisted on trying her luck with the team; Wheelock gave her a lesson, in the course of which he had to cover her hands with his as he demonstrated just how loosely to hold the reins; the touch of her fingers sent a tingling through his own. She drove with serious concentration, her fair brow puckered and her lips drawn in between her teeth, and a faint shine of perspiration across the cheek so close to Wheelock's shoulder. The horses behaved themselves and he praised her, and got her quick warm smile of pleasure.

Presently this wagon track joined the stage road, angling out of the hills to the north. Wheelock felt a swift tightening of tension, for he was reminded that, from this point, he was fair game once more for the Flaggs. They might even now be in Prineville, waiting for him; every slow and deliberate turn of the wheels could be drawing him closer to a showdown.

But he refused to spoil this pleasant time—he would deal with the problem of the Flaggs if and when he came to it. He kept the team in their collars, and the dusty miles slid past; and so, an hour before noon, they came out onto the broad canyon bottom of Crooked River, a deep hollow of land cupped by high, rimrock palisades. And presently the town itself showed ahead of them.

With plenty of room in which to do it, the town had spread out as it grew. The streets were wide, the frame houses well spaced, and nearly every yard seemed to have its own windmill flashing in the sun. Dominating everything else was the big, new wooden courthouse, over east of Main Street; and this reminded Wheelock that Prineville was the administrative seat of Crook County, and that there would be a sheriff's office here. He filed that away for future reference.

They crossed a bridge across Ochoco Creek and came in on the upper end of Main Street. Susan Telford had folded her parasol now and was sitting straight on the wagon seat, looking excitedly about her; suddenly she used the parasol as a pointer, indicating the sign on a building on the west side of the street—a brick building, oddly enough, just about the only one in this village of false-fronted wooden boxes. 'There's Allen's,' she said. 'I think that's the place we want.'

'All right,' Wheelock said, and pulled over to halt in front of the store. He wrapped the reins about the grabiron on the dash, and looked around.

A number of business houses lined the street—a hardware, a bank, and across the way a livery stable with a big frame hotel, the Jackson House, beyond it on the corner. Across the intersection he saw Poindexter's Restaurant, and a drugstore. And of course, there were the usual complement of saloons. For what it was worth, he didn't see anyone on the sidewalks that looked like a Flagg, and none of the horses standing, droopheaded, at the tie poles appeared familiar.

There were the usual sounds of a village summer day, rather startling after the stillness of the ranch on McKay Creek: voices, a dog barking, the slam of a door somewhere ... the whine of a busy sawmill.

Wheelock swung down, helped Rebecca to alight, and gave a hand to her mother. After that they all stood, a little self-conscious, and looked at one another, and the mother somehow retained her hold on Burn Wheelock's hand. She said now earnestly, 'You've been very kind. I—I don't know how to thank you.'

'Why, for what?' he demanded gruffly. 'I never done nothing. You cooked for me, and give me a place to stay. I'd say we're more than even.'

'Very well,' she said with a smile. 'But thank you just the same. I wish you the very best of luck...'

'Same to you, ma'am,' he answered earnestly. He looked at the girl, who seemed shy all at once of meeting his glance. Susan Telford gave his hand a final pat; and then they both were gone, up the steps. As they entered the store, the last he saw was a flash of that ridiculous straw hat. The door closed behind them, and he was left by himself and overwhelmed by a sudden hollow sense of loneliness.

For a moment he almost succumbed to the impulse to find some excuse for following them, but then he took himself in hand. *Don't be stupid! You got no further business with them. Bother them any more, and they'll begin to catch on to the reason. If that nice lady got the notion you were tomcatting after her daughter, she'd*

150

never let you light—and you couldn't blame her!

And so, because it was only good sense, he let them go. He turned away, to get his horse from where it was tied to the wagon tailgate.

*　　*　　*

The thing to do, he knew, was start thinking about his own affairs—and that meant thinking about the Flaggs. As he stepped into the saddle, a man came out of Hamilton's Livery and leaned his shoulders against the edge of the wide door frame, hands in the back pockets of his overalls, a wheatstraw between his jaws. The hostler's stare idly raked the street and then settled on Wheelock, and something in the way the man looked at the dun horse gave him an impulse to ride over there.

He drew up in front of the man, leaned an elbow on the horn and said, without preliminary, 'Would you happen to know this horse?'

Curiously empty black eyes lifted to his face. 'Am I supposed to?' the hostler demanded, in a voice without expression.

'I don't know. It belongs to a man named Homer Flagg. Do you know the Flaggs?'

When he waited for an answer, the other said with apparent reluctance, 'I may have seen them around.'

'Seen them today? Or a blue roan with a Star

151

brand? I traded Homer for it and I'd like to trade back.'

'No to both questions,' the man told him briefly, and pushed away from his lean to start back inside the livery.

Wheelock called after him. 'One thing more. Where in this town would I buy myself some .44 shells?'

That made the man turn again and give him a close look. But with a jerk of the head he said only, 'Gunsmith, down the next block—past Haze's saloon.'

'Thanks,' Wheelock said, and rode away leaving him there.

The gunshop was a dark cubbyhole of a building, redolent of metal and oil-soaked rags; the old man who left off working on a stripped-down rifle long enough to sell Wheelock a box of shells wore a green eyeshade, even though there seemed barely enough light at his workbench to let him see what he was doing. Wheelock paid, and returned to his waiting horse where he got the six-shooter from his blanket roll and loaded it.

He felt rather more sure of himself with the weapon recharged and tucked into his waistband, under the front of the jacket. Actually, though, his fear of running into the Flaggs had been eased considerably. Apparently they weren't here in Prineville; he began to believe that, having lost him, they'd taken the body of Chet and gone home to make a report to the rest of the clan.

He had no illusions, however. The killing of Chet Flagg changed everything. Because of that, he was in real danger as long as he remained in country where any of that brood might lay hands on him. Perhaps he had best forget his intention of looking for a job here in the Ochoco. Safest to keep riding as far as the worn-out dun horse would carry him—down into Nevada, maybe, or over into Idaho.

But, damn it! A man purely hated to admit he was running!

As he debated, he became aware of currents of sound flowing through the propped-open doors of Haze's saloon, nearby. Though not in any real sense a drinking man, like any cowboy Burn Wheelock appreciated a shot on occasion; and it suddenly occurred to him now that over a filled glass was the proper place to consider his problem. Also, a saloon was the clearinghouse of the range country—if there were riding jobs available in the vicinity of Prineville, there would be word of it here. So he retied the knot he had just loosened in the reins, and left his horse with a couple of other animals at Haze's hitchrack.

A saloon was the social club of a male frontier; any man who had the price of a drink—and who was not an Indian, a sheepherder, or some other undesirable— could make himself welcome and find some measure of escape from the loneliness of a mostly empty land. Whether the bar was a marvel of carved cherrywood and beveled mirrors, or merely a pine plank laid across a couple of barrels, the function was the same; and so were the smells of whiskey and beer and horse and sweat and wet sawdust, and the familiar confusion of men's voices oiled by what they had been drinking.

Entering, Wheelock found the normal noontime sprinkling of townsmen, and of others in off the range. A cluster around a table toward the rear were watching a card game that seemed to have been of some hours' duration, to judge from the blue cloud of tobacco smoke that swam beneath the rafters. Satisfied by a first sweeping survey of the room that none of these men were Flaggs, Burn Wheelock eased up unobtrusively to a place at the end of the bar and waited to be served.

The bartender on duty—cadaverously lean, bald, with a drooping mustache—seemed to be Gil Haze himself. The man must be something of a musician, for a fiddle and bow held a prominent position on the backbar; but hanging from its trigger guard, on a nail, Wheelock also saw a silver-handled six-shooter, indicating that the saloonkeeper had other accomplishments. He came mopping his way down the counter now and Wheelock ordered beer. Haze drew it from a spigot, knocked off the foam, and scooped up the dime Wheelock laid out on the polished wood.

154

He said casually, 'Don't think you've been in before.'

'No,' Wheelock said. 'Maybe you could tell me if any of the cattle outfits hereabouts are hiring crew?'

The saloonkeeper thought it over. 'I ain't heard of any in particular. But this time of year, there's always the chance somebody could use another hand. Was I you, I'd just drift on up the canyon. You might catch on almost any place.'

'Thanks,' Wheelock said, and took a drag at his beer as Haze turned away, about his business. The idle run of voices continued; through the open door came the unsynchronized pounding of hammers, where workmen were putting up a building of some kind on a vacant lot across the street.

Without warning, an eruption of angry voices broke out at the rear of the room in the vicinity of the poker game. All other talk ceased at once. Setting down his beer glass, Wheelock turned but could make out little more than the backs of men crowded about the table, and the blue cloud of smoke hanging over them. The shouting had subsided quickly, to a tense exchange that was too subdued for Wheelock to hear what the quarrel was about. But now someone had left the group around the table and was hurrying to lean both hands on the bar as, in an anxious voice, he told the saloonkeeper, 'Better get over there, Gil. It looks like trouble. Telford, and that gambler from Boise...'

Haze swore, flung down his mop rag and started along the duck boards toward the counter's end. Wheelock, gaping, found his voice: 'Telford? *Reub* Telford?' He got a sour nod from Haze, but as the latter came around past him the young fellow pivoted and caught him by a sleeve. 'But I'd heard—I mean, someone told me he was gone somewhere on business...'

'Well, he's back, then.' Haze jerked his arm free. 'Been around town a couple of days— most of the time, right at that table!' He was headed that way, then, and with only a second's hesitation Burn Wheelock went after him.

He let the gaunt man elbow a way for them toward the crowd at the table. It gave room and now, past Haze's shoulder, Wheelock had a look at the cardplayers.

Of the five seated about the oilcloth-covered table, with its scatter of coins and bills and cardboards, all but two were keeping quiet— eyes alert and empty hands in plain sight on the oilcloth covering. They were watching the pair who seemed to be held as though locked into a frozen tableau of conflict. One of these Burn Wheelock passed over quickly enough, guessing from his appearance and from the bowler hat set above his pale and chiseled face that he must be the gambler from Boise.

The fifth man, directly across the table from him, would be Susan Telford's husband.

Wheelock hardly knew what he expected; what he saw was a stocky figure in brown corduroy jacket, and a blue-striped shirt buttoned at the throat but without a collar or tie. The man's broad face was ruddy of complexion, his hair and whiskers the yellow color of new rope. He would probably be fifty but the flesh of his face looked smooth and unwrinkled; only the pouches forming below his black eyes, and the sagging of his throat, betrayed his age.

Looking at him, Wheelock supposed he might have seemed almost a handsome fellow. Moreover, he had a domineering set to his mouth and it was easy to see how a woman as unsure of herself—and as lacking in ballast—as Susan Telford might have thought that here was a man whose strength she could rest on. But Burn Wheelock, already inclined to dislike him, thought he noticed other things in that broad, blunt face. Or, rather, the things that weren't there.

Or so it appeared to him, in that brief moment when he had his one and only clear view of the man's face, glaring in anger at the one seated opposite. And then that other man said something, too low for Wheelock's ears to catch; but whatever, it had its effect on Reub Telford. There was the scrape of chair legs and suddenly Telford was stumbling to his feet, rearing up into the drift of blue tobacco smoke, backing from the table. And as he moved, one hand pawed at the skirt of his corduroy jacket and a gun appeared in it.

So far as Wheelock could see, the other man made no move at all; but there was a burst of smoke and flame and, before his horrified stare, a small black hole appeared just over the bridge of Reub Telford's nose. His hand opened, the gun dropped to the floor unfired.

And then Telford struck the wall behind him and began sliding slowly down it, as the pulsing crack of the gambler's gun hung upon the room.

CHAPTER TWELVE

The room went still. Wheelock judged that every one of these dozen men was just as shocked and stunned as he was. The cardplayers sat frozen in their chairs; only the man who had done the killing seemed unconcerned—his sallow gambler's face impassive, the little gun waiting in case it should be needed again.

Gil Haze was the first to break free. He swore and walked around the table, shoving men out of his way, and leaned to look at the dead man. When he straightened his face was bleak and angry. He looked coldly at the gambler.

'Well, he's dead enough. You got him right between the eyes!'

'That's where I aimed,' the other answered coolly.

Haze leaned again and picked up the gun that had dropped, unfired, from the dead man's fingers. He rolled the cylinder out and spun it, checking the loads; snapped it shut and let the hammer off cock. Turning then to one of the silent bystanders he said, 'Al, how about seeing can you get some law here? If you don't find the marshal, then check if there's anybody in the sheriff's office at the courthouse.'

Al nodded and started away, still looking over his shoulder as though reluctant to leave a scene where something was going on. The one who had done the killing showed some emotion for the first time; his head had lifted sharply and he told the saloonowner, 'Don't try to make this something more than it was. Every man who saw it will bear witness. He was the first to draw.'

A number of heads worked up and down jerkily. 'Telford opened the ball, all right,' someone said, and another agreed, 'Wasn't much else to do but kill him.'

Haze ignored them. 'What's your name?' he demanded, still narrowly observing the gambler.

The latter hesitated as though he preferred not to give it, then shrugged and answered shortly, 'Dunning.'

'Well, Dunning,' the saloonkeeper said. 'I don't like killings in my place of business, under any circumstances. Maybe you better tell me how it happened.'

'He was trying to deal seconds,' the other replied. 'And he wasn't much good. I spotted him for a tinhorn when I first sat in the game, but I gave him time to get careless.'

'He dropped a card,' one of the players volunteered. 'It couldn't have been plainer.'

Gil Haze thought this over, and then shrugged.

If anyone felt regret over the death of a man who had been their neighbor, Burn Wheelock could detect few signs of it. Now Gil Haze shoved the dead man's gun behind his apron; as though that meant the matter was settled, Dunning's gun disappeared into his clothing and he began methodically gathering up the coins and bills that lay in front of him. The other players began to do the same. The poker game, apparently, was over. A muttering of talk began.

Someone said, 'Telford had some money on the table. Who gets it?'

'His widow!'

Heads lifted and turned as Burn Wheelock moved up to the table, jarred out of his stunned role of onlooker. He felt coldly curious stares rest on him; the player who had started to reach for the greenbacks lying at Telford's vacated place drew his hand back and demanded, 'Who the hell are *you*? And what's this about a widow?'

'The fellow's right,' Gil Haze answered him. 'Come to think of it. Or at least, I heard a few months back that Telford had him a new missus he'd brought out from Kansas City or such place—a woman with a grown daughter. I never seen either of them. He took them out to his place without even making a stop in town, and far as I know they ain't been back.'

'They are now,' Burn Wheelock told him. 'I rode in by way of Telford's, and I met 'em. They asked me to bring them in to Prineville. I left them up the street, at Allen's store.'

'You don't say!'

Haze was gathering Telford's money. 'I'll deliver this to the sheriff; it'll be up to him to see the lady gets it.' He shook his head. 'Somebody ought to tell her what's happened to her husband. But—*who*? Nobody even knows her!'

Wheelock drew a breath, and settled his shoulders. 'Looks like my job,' he said, in resignation. 'I know her. I'll do the telling...'

*　　*　　*

He paused a long moment before Allen's brick-front mercantile, staring miserably at the ranch wagon and team still tied out in the street while a dozen still-born notions for delivering his

161

awful message tumbled fruitlessly through his head. Squaring his shoulders, he turned to the glass doors and got one of them open before he could change his mind.

A bell jangled on its spring. As he pushed the door to with his heel he looked about a room that had tall, narrow windows, a pressed-tin ceiling, shelves and counters stacked high with all kinds of merchandise and so narrowly crowding the floor that there seemed scarcely room to walk through. Toward the back he could see Susan Telford engaged in serious conversation with a fussy-looking, graying man whom he judged to be the storekeeper himself; nearer, a sales clerk was showing Rebecca some hand-painted lampshades, but somehow Wheelock got the impression she was scarcely listening. Her anxious attention seemed centered on what her mother was doing.

She glanced his way at the sound of the bell, and he caught her quick look of surprise at seeing him again. Wheelock, for his part, could have asked nothing better than a chance to have a word with the girl, without her mother hearing. He went directly to her.

'Why, hello, Mr Wheelock,' she greeted him. She introduced the young man beside her. 'This is Ned Hershel. He's Mr Allen's assistant.'

His clerk, you mean, Wheelock thought as he gave the man the shortest of nods. Somehow he

162

knew he was not going to like Ned Hershel. He was a ruddy-cheeked young man, his brown hair already thinning; he was neatly dressed in a sharply cut business suit, with a four-in-hand and a high stiff collar, and he had a businessman's eager, easy smile and—so it seemed to Wheelock—entirely too active an interest in Rebecca Savage.

Wheelock pointedly ignored him, after that first unfriendly nod. Turning to the girl he began, 'Your mother—'

'I'm afraid there's bad news,' she told him, and he detected bitterness in her voice. 'Mr Allen doesn't seem to want to let us have any supplies. It begins to look as though Reub Telford's credit isn't good in this town.' She acted as though she weren't too surprised to learn it.

Burn Wheelock drew a deep breath. He glanced at Ned Hershel, standing at the girl's elbow and listening to every word of this with a fatuous grin pasted on his face—he wished he could tell the man to go somewhere and get lost. In any event this had to be said while he had the girl out of earshot of her mother, so he went doggedly ahead with it.

'I'm afraid I got worse news than that. Telford's dead—he was killed, not half an hour ago, in a saloon down the street.'

He heard her gasp. 'Dead!' she echoed. 'Are—are you *sure*?'

'I saw it. There was an argument over a card

163

game.' And he proceeded to tell her while Hershel, his mouth agape, swung his head back and forth in that damned high collar. Finished, Wheelock saw such desolation in the girl's face that he was unable to keep from placing a hand on her shoulder and—hardly aware that he called her by name—exclaiming, 'Rebecca, I'm sorry! Is there anything—?'

She shook her head. 'I'm all right,' she insisted. 'But—poor Mama!'

'He's down at Haze's,' Wheelock went on. 'Lying on the floor. Somebody went to fetch the law.'

Rebecca was staring down at her hands, that were knotted tightly together. She shook her head and said, in a dead tone, 'I'm sorry, but I can't seem to feel one way or the other about Reub Telford. But—oh, poor Mama!' she said again, in anguish. 'How will we ever tell her?'

'She's heading this way,' Wheelock warned her softly.

'Oh, dear!' Rebecca straightened her shoulders. 'Well, it can't be put off...'

Susan appeared troubled and confused. She looked at Wheelock almost as though she didn't recognize him; she turned helplessly to her daughter and exclaimed, with a shake of her head, 'Mr Allen says it's no use, he positively won't let us have anything on credit. I can't prove who I am, for one thing—but, it's more than that. He's had trouble getting Reuben to pay his bills, even when there was

164

reason to believe he had money in his pocket. It seems there's a big balance owing and Mr Allen won't add to it.' She showed her hurt and bewilderment. 'I just don't understand. It makes me feel like—like a *beggar!*'

Wheelock saw the girl steel herself. She took her mother's arm. 'Mama—' she began determinedly. And at that moment the bell over the door jangled again into life.

The man who entered was tall and spare, in his early thirties perhaps, with a face weathered nearly as dark as the drooping mustache that bracketed his mouth. His appearance, and his brush-scarred clothing, suggested a cattleman; but the piece of metal pinned to his shirt, where the front of his coat nearly hid it, was a sheriff's star. Closing the door behind him, he gave the group a careful study. 'Which of you ladies—' he began, then appeared to settle on the older woman and came directly to her. 'Ma'am, I'm Sheriff Jim Blake.' He touched finger to hatbrim. 'I guess you must be the widow.'

'*Widow?*' she echoed, and her face drained white.

In alarm, Burn Wheelock thought she was about to faint, and so did Rebecca apparently for she tightened her grip protectively on her mother's arm; but Susan seemed to be made of stouter stuff than that. After all—as Wheelock suddenly reminded himself—it was not her first time to be informed she had suddenly, and tragically, been left without a husband. She

165

stared at the lawman, shock reflected in her whole expression. It was the sheriff's turn to stammer a little, taken aback by what he read there.

'You mean—you weren't *told*? But I thought—'

'I meant to,' Wheelock answered him. 'You didn't give me the time to figure how to break it.' He added bitterly, 'It's sure as hell broken now, anyway!'

Blake appeared nonplussed. He looked at the woman again and could only say, lamely, 'I'm sorry.'

She had control of herself, though she was still as pale as death. 'About my husband,' she said now in a shaken voice. 'Won't *someone* tell me? Please!'

Wheelock did, as briefly and as gently as he could. He thought she took it very well, though Rebecca held close to her and kept an anxious look on her face. Afterward the sheriff confirmed Wheelock's account, saying, 'That seems to have been the way of it, ma'am. I've had him carried to the undertaker's.'

'What about the one who killed him?' Burn Wheelock put in. 'That fellow Dunning?'

'I had to let him go,' the other answered—a shade defensively, he thought. 'There were too many witnesses ready to swear Reub Telford tried to cheat, and then pulled a gun when he got caught at it. Since Dunning shot in self-defense, I had no excuse to lay him under

166

arrest.' But there was a glint of steel in the sheriff's eye as he added, 'I did suggest he better find him another town. This is the first killing Prineville's had since we kicked the Vigilantes out, and it don't sit well. I think Dunning took the hint. If I ain't mistaken, he's already gone.'

'Just as well,' Burn Wheelock agreed shortly.

Jim Blake reached into a coat pocket. 'A few personal things I found on the body,' he told Susan. 'And the money he had in the game. They belong to you.' He brought the items out one by one and laid them on the edge of a counter—a cheap-looking silver watch, a small stack of coins, and finally a sweated and shapeless leather wallet.

Rebecca picked this up and opened it; she said, in some astonishment, 'Why, there's almost two hundred dollars in here! So at least,' she added, looking directly at Allen, 'we should be able now to pay for our groceries!'

The storekeeper reddened. He turned hastily, appealing to Reub Telford's widow. 'Please! I can't tell you how sorry I am about this—and embarrassed, too! But after all, I *am* a businessman; and the account in question—'

'I think we're beginning to see,' Rebecca interpreted bleakly, 'that Reub Telford didn't have much of a reputation in Prineville!'

'That's of no matter, now,' Walter Allen insisted. 'Mrs Telford, naturally I'll be pleased

167

to fill your order. And if you'd like a little time, I'm sure that can be arranged.'

'Thank you. But—' Susan passed a hand irresolutely across her cheek. 'Really, I—I'm so confused. I don't quite know what I'm doing.'

They all looked at her, Rebecca with anxious concern. And because it had to be said, Burn Wheelock reluctantly broke an awkward silence by pointing out, 'Something's going to have to be done about a funeral...'

'Excuse *me*, ma'am.' Almost as though that were his cue, Ned Hershel was pushing forward eagerly. He told Susan, 'I'd be most honored to handle that matter. My uncle,' he went on to explain quickly, at her puzzled look, 'is the Methodist minister here. Between us I'm sure we can take care of all the details—just tell me where you want it to be, and when.'

Susan turned helplessly to her daughter, and Rebecca took the decision in her own hands. 'I see no reason to put it off. We've noticed the cemetery, on the hill north of town. It seems a pleasant place. And under the circumstances, there doesn't really need to be a church service.'

'The cemetery, then. At two o'clock?' the young fellow suggested. 'That should give plenty of time. I'll see that everything's taken care of.'

'Thank you,' the girl exclaimed. 'Thank you so very much!'

168

'Only too glad to help. That is—' Ned Hershel looked at his employer. 'If Mr Allen can spare me for an hour...' He got a wave of the hand in dismissal, and was off at once about his mission.

The warm smile of gratitude from Rebecca, that he took with him, made Burn Wheelock just as pleased to see him leave. Jealousy caused Wheelock to speak a trifle more gruffly than he meant to. 'With him in charge,' he said, 'looks like you wouldn't be needing *me* no longer...' But at that, the older woman stirred from her dazed silence and, rather surprisingly, caught at his hand with both of hers.

She said earnestly, '*You'll* come this afternoon, Mr Wheelock?'

'To the burying?'

'We'd both appreciate it. I think of you now as our friend. It will make it seem less lonely...'

'Well—' He hesitated, self-conscious under her urging—and all at once aware that the sheriff was looking at him with an odd expression. 'Well, sure,' he said. 'If you'd really like me there.' And then, seeing how wan and pale she looked, he added a suggestion: 'Why don't the two of you let me get a room for you, across the street at the hotel? You can have something to eat and rest till two o'clock.'

Surprisingly enough, it was the storekeeper who vetoed that. 'Absolutely not!' he said indignantly, 'Mrs Allen would never hear of such a thing! You ladies come home with me.

You'll take dinner with us, and we can make you much more comfortable than in some hotel room. I really insist!'

He seemed in earnest; Burn Wheelock had an impression he wanted to make up for his earlier behavior about refusing credit. Rebecca, for one, seemed ready to take his offer—she must have felt her mother needed a friendlier atmosphere, just then, than she was apt to find at the Jackson House. 'It's very kind of you,' she told Allen. 'We'll be obliged to accept.'

'Two o'clock, then,' Wheelock told the women. As he turned to leave Allen's he didn't much like the way Sheriff Blake wheeled slowly and watched him go. The lawman's stare seemed to rest on him like a weight.

CHAPTER THIRTEEN

The scene at the cemetery, when he rode up shortly before two o'clock, was a surprise to Wheelock. He'd expected it to be a bleak and lonely business for the women, but he could see rigs and saddle horses tied along the fence and perhaps two dozen people already making their way among the graves and headboards, or gathered beside the raw, new hole and mound of earth. As he walked across the grass to join them he noticed the plain pine coffin

170

being lifted down out of the undertaker's wagon, the parson waiting with Bible in hand, Ned Hershel bustling about and giving everyone orders. The two workmen who had dug the grave stood by at a respectful distance, with shovels ready to cover it again.

Wheelock picked out one or two faces he knew—Gil Haze from the saloon, and Jim Blake accompanying a pretty young woman he decided must be the sheriff's wife. He wondered why they were all here, at this burying of a man none of them had known or bothered about. Out of curiosity, perhaps—to stare at Reub Telford's widow and stepdaughter; the thought stirred quick resentment in him. But as he looked at them—and especially when he saw the bunch of flowers someone had brought from his own front yard to lay upon the coffin—Wheelock had some second thoughts.

A two-seated buggy and team was last to arrive up the road from town, Walter Allen handling the reins. When it pulled up at the gate, young Hershel was there to help Rebecca and her mother down. Mrs Allen had come too, an austere little woman but apparently capable of kindness—Wheelock saw how she took her place at Susan's elbow, ready if she was needed.

He thought Susan was actually taken aback at the sight of so many people. She looked about with a wondering expression; Burn

171

Wheelock hoped she, too, could understand that these people were here from a sense of compassion.

Prineville was not a big enough town that death could be taken as an impersonal matter. In that sparsely settled land, anyone's loss—even a stranger's—deserved sympathy and a show of solidarity with those who were left. It was as plain as that.

The black-coated parson had stepped forward to meet the women and lead them to their place, and Burn Wheelock found room for himself in the rough circle that formed about the grave. Hands folded, the warm breeze tugging at his hair—unlike these other men, he had no hat to remove—he listened to the preacher's words and watched Rebecca's solemn face. He thought the straw hat with the cherries looked pathetically out of place on such an occasion—when she put it on that morning, Rebecca had never suspected where she would end up wearing it.

Ned Hershel had managed to station himself close beside her, attentive and all too ready to prove helpful. Wheelock was willing to bet he'd have put a sympathetic arm about her shoulders, had he thought he could get away with it.

It was, in a way, an oddly pleasant setting for such a purpose as this. The winy sunlight lay upon the stillness, caught within the wide bowl of the palisaded canyon bottom. Out in the flats, a meadowlark sang over and over.

Abruptly the thing was over. The box had been lowered, the ropes that held it flipped free, and the crowd solemnly dispersed to let the gravediggers finish their task. A few people lingered to speak to Rebecca and Susan, strangers though they were, and from the look on Susan's face it was plain how deeply moved she was by such unexpected sympathy. Someone had given her the flowers from the coffin; it was touching to see the way she held them. 'Thank you,' Wheelock heard her say to Sheriff Blake's young wife. 'You're very kind. All of you...'

One of the last to approach was a portly and prosperous-appearing man, with silver-white mustache and side whiskers and a businessman's shrewd glance. As he took Susan's hand Wheelock heard him introduce himself—Henry Mortonson, from the Prineville bank. 'I heard about you from Sheriff Blake, Mrs Telford. I wanted to pay my respects. It's a poor time to discuss business, but there *is* a matter of your husband's account. The balance is rather sizable, you know—something close to four thousand dollars...'

'That—much?' Susan looked as though she would faint. But then, it would have been just like Reub Telford not to have bothered informing her there was money in the bank—a man who would leave her stranded and penniless while he gambled in saloons, and let his bills pile up even when he had money available to pay his creditors.

'Do you know if he left a will?' Mortonson asked. When she shook her head, he went on, 'That can entail a certain amount of red tape—advertising for relatives for claims against the estate, and so on; I'll be glad to handle the legal details. The court should be able to turn the residue over to you in fairly short order. A week or two, perhaps—I'll get word to you. Meanwhile, if you should need anything feel free to come and see me. Something can be arranged, I'm sure.' He gave her a banker's smile and was gone about his business.

When the storekeeper and his wife escorted the two women toward the cemetery gate, Wheelock trailed after them hoping for a chance to speak with Rebecca. Standing in the sun beside the carriage and team, Walter Allen said, 'You *will* stay with us tonight, of course?'

But Susan shook her head. 'We really can't. We've been enough of a bother to you already. Oh, but we have,' she insisted over Mrs Allen's protest. 'Besides, I—I wouldn't feel right, just now—underfoot in another woman's house. I think I'd like to go home.'

'Home?' Rebecca repeated in a tone of surprise. 'You mean—to the ranch?'

Her mother nodded. 'So much has happened—there's so much to think about—I feel I could cope best under my own roof. I do

174

hope you understand,' she pleaded with the Allens.

'Whatever you say, Mrs Telford,' the storekeeper assured her. 'Though you know you're welcome.' He added, 'But, didn't you tell us there's no one now to run the place for you, or even do the chores? How can two women get along without any kind of help?'

'Oh, I know we'll manage,' she said. 'Perhaps—' She was looking around, as though searching for someone, until she caught sight of Burn Wheelock in the background. At once she came to him and looked directly into his face. 'Mr Wheelock, I wouldn't want to impose—but you did say you were looking for a job. *Would* you consider staying on, a month or two at least—to give us time to make permanent plans? You might have to wait a little for your wages, but it does look as though I'd be able to pay you something...'

She had caught him completely by surprise. He could only stare at her for a moment; suddenly there was nothing he would have liked better, but a warning voice said: *Go slow! There are some reasons you can't do it—and all of them named Flagg!* She sensed his hesitation, she touched his hand and said, 'Please.'

Wheelock swallowed. He looked around him, saw Ned Hershel frowning as though he had bitten into something that tasted bad. And there was Sheriff Blake, studying him with the

175

same narrow look that had so disturbed him earlier.

But then his glance met Rebecca's and he knew that, wise or not, his mind had been made up for him. He pushed rope-hardened fingers through hair that was tangled by the wind, and nodded. 'Why, sure,' he said, turning again to Susan. 'If you really think I can be a help—I reckon I could stick around awhile, anyway, Be glad to.'

'Thank you,' she said.

Walter Allen accepted the decision graciously enough. 'Very well,' he said, all brisk efficiency. 'You'll be wanting those supplies, then. Drop in and we'll take you down to the store, and Ned can fill the order for you. Just be sure you've asked for everything you need—I can't send you away with anything less...'

*   *   *

Filling the order turned out a time-consuming business, with young Hershel attempting to be helpful and Rebecca and her mother carefully debating the need of every item. Wheelock grew impatient. Trying to hurry the process, he began carrying things out one by one and stowing them in the wagon. Finally, however, as he returned from toting a sack of flour on his shoulder he decided the transaction was finished.

Susan was moving toward the door, chatting with the storekeeper; but Ned Hershel had detained the girl and seemed to be trying to hold her with talk for as long as he could. Scowling, Wheelock drifted over to a counter stacked with shirts and jeans, and other items of men's clothing. As he poked around the merchandise he narrowly eyed what was happening yonder.

When Hershel took Rebecca's hand, earnestly talking while he stood holding it, Burn Wheelock finally decided things had gone far enough. 'You got any other hats besides these?' he demanded, raising his voice. 'None of them fit me.'

He thought the young fellow would gladly have throttled him; but with his boss listening, Hershel had to remember he was a clerk with the duty of waiting on customers. He said, not very enthusiastically, 'I'll see what's in the stock room...'

It took him some minutes. When he returned carrying a stack of wide-brimmed range hats, Rebecca had gone to join her mother and Allen in the doorway and Hershel couldn't help but see that his intimate moment with the girl had ended. In a poor temper, he had to wait as the other man took his time about choosing a headpiece, to replace the one that had been lost a couple of nights ago. 'This should do,' Wheelock said finally, as he carefully shaped four dents into its crown. The clerk only

177

grunted.

Rebecca and Susan were leaving. Ned Hershel plainly wanted to go after them but Wheelock was of no mind to let him. 'I almost forgot,' he added pleasantly. 'I need some hardware. A couple of heavy-duty door hinges.' With a look of angry despair, Hershel motioned him to another counter where Wheelock found what he wanted to repair the sagging barn door. He had already picked out an extra shirt and pair of jeans; altogether these purchases very nearly depleted what was left of the pay he'd got from Youngdahl.

The money he counted out was accepted glumly. 'Think you're pretty clever, don't you, cowboy!' Hershel said in a voice that fairly trembled. 'I'm not going to forget this!' He hadn't missed what the other was up to; he was really angry. Wheelock, with a shrug, turned his back and walked out of the store, shoving the hardware he'd bought into a pocket of his jacket.

The women were ready, having a last word with Walter Allen. After a check of the knot anchoring his dun to the tailgate, Wheelock untied the team and climbed up beside Rebecca. He yelled the horses into motion, but once they were rolling out of town a silence fell on all three people on the wagon's high seat—a silence, he thought, that reflected the shattering change that had occurred in the last, fateful hours...

On the steps of the Jackson House, Sheriff Jim Blake stood and watched the wagon go; he wore a scowl of narrow speculation as he sucked at a tooth and wondered about the wisdom of letting those people out of his sight. He was still debating when he swung down the steps and rounded the corner of Third Street, heading away from Main toward the new courthouse.

But he had his opinion, and it seemed valid; once a judgment was formed, Blake tended to stick by it. So now he remained satisfied with this one. When he reached his office, he relieved the deputy on duty, scaled his hat onto a wall hook and settled himself at his desk. He rummaged in a pigeonhole until he found the letter he was looking for. Having reread it, the sheriff took pen and ink and in a firm, bold hand wrote his reply, while the sounds of the village came on the drift of warm air through an open window at his elbow.

Dear Sam:

There is a man named Wheelock working on the Telford place here, north of Prineville. No question in my mind but what he's the one you asked me to keep a watch for.

I haven't placed him under arrest because he seems to me certain to stay put where he is, at least for the time being. Let me know your pleasure regarding same.

Jim Blake signed the letter, addressed an envelope for it, affixed a stamp with a solid blow of a fist. He dropped the envelope onto a pile of outgoing mail, destined for the next morning's stage northbound for The Dalles.

*   *   *

Across the litter of the supper table, Burn Wheelock said, 'While I was killing time in town this afternoon, I went over to the recorder's office at the courthouse. It was none of my business; but I felt you didn't actually know what you've got here, and it struck me somebody ought to look it up.'

'And what did you find out?' Rebecca asked.

'Well, it looks pretty good. Reub Telford owned clear title to a half section, including this land the house stands on, a stretch of the creek, some good timber, and the haymeadow along the bottom. And, of course, there's all the hill range available that a spread this size could need to run cattle on.

'But Telford sure as the devil never did much with it—in fact, I can't see why he wanted a ranch at all.' Wheelock frowned. 'Unless maybe he was using it as a cover.'

'A cover?' Susan repeated in a puzzled tone.

'What he means, Mama,' her daughter answered bleakly, 'is that it looks as though Reub Telford was a gambler and a crook; no one in Prineville seems to be sure what else! It's

180

not a pleasant thing,' she admitted, 'but if it happens to be true, then I think we should face up to it.'

Looking at Susan's expression, Burn Wheelock thought he had never felt so sorry for anyone. Her lips began to tremble; dropping her glance to the hands that lay twisted together on the tabletop, she said slowly, 'I married a stranger. That's the honest truth! I should have known better, but—I was so tired of fighting. I couldn't lean on Becky forever. I wanted this to be the solution I hoped for—I wanted it too much!'

'You mustn't blame yourself,' her daughter said earnestly. Susan tried to thank her with a smile. She seemed to have aged, within these last few hours.

Wheelock shifted in his chair. He cleared his throat, determined to change the subject. 'Naturally I ain't the one to say,' he began, 'but looks to me you're in good shape here. This place your husband left you needs work, but it's got the makings of a pretty fair little ranch in the hands of the right party. No reason you couldn't sell it, just as it stands, for enough to go back to Omaha and make yourself a new start.

'Or,' he went on, as no one spoke, 'with four thousand in your account, that banker sounds like he could be talked into lending you enough more, using the ranch as collateral, to stock it and run it yourself.'

'You really think we could make a go of it?' Rebecca asked dubiously.

He nodded. 'But it don't sound like that's an idea that would have much appeal for your mother.'

The older woman was watching her daughter's face. She said now, slowly, 'I think you like Oregon, Becky.'

'Yes, I honestly do,' the girl admitted. 'It's been like a whole new life. In fact—well, I've sort of fallen in love with this spot here on the creek—the mountains, and that marvelous sky. I honestly don't think, of my own choice, I'd want to go back. But of course,' she added hastily, 'it's up to you, Mama.'

The older woman sighed, and shook her head. And then, to Wheelock's astonishment, he heard her answer: 'To be truthful, I don't feel I'd have anything to go back to. I had no friends there—nothing but hard memories. But those people we met in town today—somehow, I had a feeling they wanted to be neighborly, that somehow I was already one of them. That'—she seemed to grope for words—'that I almost *belong*.'

'Do you mean,' Rebecca demanded, as though she couldn't believe it, 'you might actually consider *staying*?'

'It would depend, of course,' Susan said quickly. 'On our finding someone to manage the ranch for us—someone who knows about buying stock, and hiring men, and all the

182

things Mr Wheelock was just telling us.' Her look sought Burn Wheelock's face, then. 'Of course, if *he* might be willing to take on the job...'

He couldn't answer immediately. Stalling for time, he drained his coffee cup and set it down and pushed it away from him. The two women were looking at him, waiting. Wheelock took a breath, knowing what he had to do. 'Look!' he blurted. 'You're putting a lot of trust in somebody you don't really know. I'll be dead level with you. I'm pretty sure I could do a job—I'm a top-flight buckaroo, if I say it myself. But—there's some things about me you have a right to be told.

'I rode in here yesterday morning,' he went on, blundering ahead with it, 'on a crow-bait horse, didn't even own an outfit. I told you I'd been waylaid and robbed, but that ain't exactly the whole story. Truth is, the men that jumped me had more on their minds than robbery. I'd had some trouble with them, up at Antelope. They trailed me from there.'

The girl and her mother exchanged a startled glance. It was Rebecca who asked, 'Does this—trouble—have anything to do with Mama and me?'

'It could. That's why you better hear the whole story.' And resolutely he laid the story out for them—all of it, from the hanging of Rufe Flagg, to the deadly events at his camp in the Ochocos. He held back any mention, by

183

name, of Harper Youngdahl, or of Jess Croy or the other Y-Bar riders involved in Rufe's lynching. That was something he didn't think they needed to know.

When he finished, there was a stillness. At last Susan said, 'I don't think I understand. The hanging was a very dreadful thing. But couldn't you have explained it to the law, the way you did just now? That the whole thing was that foreman's doing, and not your employer's nor anyone else's...'

'Yes, Burn,' the girl agreed earnestly. 'Don't you feel somehow, you haven't helped the situation?'

He shrugged, beginning to be a little angry—it might have been because they didn't understand, or perhaps because he suspected they might be right. 'I did what I thought I had to. When I hire out to work for a brand, I've always believed in giving it my loyalty.'

'Nobody could blame you for that,' Rebecca insisted. 'But if you had stayed and had the matter out—'

'I know what you're gonna tell me! The Flaggs wouldn't have been camped on my tail, and I wouldn't have had to kill one of them. Well, it's too late now. Chet Flagg's dead—and I will be too, if any of his kin ever set eyes on me. So there's no going back now.

'Before we decide if I'm to work for you,' he finished, 'you had to know all this. It's my problem, but I wouldn't like to think of it

184

following me down here and maybe getting you two involved. So—I leave it up to you.'

Rebecca looked directly into his eyes. 'But what do *you* think?'

He wanted to be very sure of his answer. He said finally, 'I've been figuring that if the Flaggs should get as far south as Prineville, I ought to be able to keep out of their way. Anyhow, I'm willing to take the risk if you are.'

'It's just that we'd feel perfectly terrible,' Susan said, 'if anything should happen to you—just because you stayed on here to help us...'

'I don't think it will,' Burn Wheelock assured her.

Suddenly he felt good, with a decision made—the decision he had really wanted. He leaned back in his chair, both palms propped against the table's edge, and looked from one to the other of the women. 'If we're agreed,' he said, 'then we've got some planning to do!'

CHAPTER FOURTEEN

They had a lot of planning to do. The women were delighted, of course, with Wheelock's suggestion that a windmill could be installed to bring creek water right in to a hand pump at the kitchen sink; but that was something for the future. So were such matters as stocking the

185

range and hiring extra hands: These would all have to wait on word from Henry Mortonson that Reub Telford's estate had cleared, and cash and credit were available. A week or two, the banker had said—an impatient time, here on high country range where summers ran short and the season was already advancing. But it wasn't a process to be hurried by wishing for it.

There were things that *could* be done, however. Of first priority, Wheelock decided, was fixing the roof of the house—he didn't have to see the stains on the ceiling to know that it must leak torrents during the occasional hard mountain storms.

Accordingly, he felled and trimmed a cedar, rived out a batch of shakes, and spent the good part of a day crawling around on the slanted rooftop patching the spots that needed it, with the aid of flattened tins for flashing. He found himself thoroughly enjoying being occupied once more with useful labor—working up a sweat under the warm sun, surrounded by the sweet clean smell of the split cedar.

Next, the barn...

That broken door, scraping and wobbling on its remaining hinge, was an affront to his sense of neatness and to the appearance of the whole ranchyard. Working in what was left of fading evening light, he got it rehung on the hardware he'd brought from Prineville the day before. Afterward, as he put his tools away and finished his chores by grainy dusk, he had the satisfactory feeling of a good day's work accomplished.

To set his own tasks and lay out his own schedule, without someone handing out orders, was a new experience. He had to admit that he liked it.

One thing disturbed him. Lying on his cot that night, trying to get to sleep but too keenly aware of Becky's presence in the adjoining room, he knew that some different sleeping arrangement needed to be found. He had no business spending his nights in the house. Later, if they began to hire crew, there would be time enough to think about putting up a bunkshack; but with Wheelock the only hand, it would serve if he fixed up quarters in a corner of the barn. The women might protest; still, he couldn't help but feel they would be more comfortable having the house to themselves again. Surely, if anything should happen and they needed him in a hurry, he would be within close enough call.

So the next morning found him with the newly mended doors propped open, and his sleeves rolled up for the job of putting the barn in some kind of order. Before anything else could be done, the neglected mess in the half-dozen stalls had to have attention—and there was no more distasteful job for a man who judged himself a top-hand buckaroo. Already he could begin to see the less pleasant side of being one's own boss; it meant, even though you were boss, you had nobody else to delegate the unwelcome chores to. With a sigh of resignation he went at it.

At the end of an hour of sweating labor, he was trundling a loaded wheelbarrow through the wide doorway when he caught sight of a buggy with a black top and shining yellow wheels, spinning along the road beyond the creek. There was a handsome, high-stepping sorrel horse between the shafts. He halted, setting the wheelbarrow down as he watched to see if the rig would pass the Telford place.

It did not. It turned in, and wheels and hoofs made a small thunder as they took the plank bridge spanning McKay Creek. Standing there in the doorway, he tried with puckered frown to make out the indistinct shape of the one perched on the buggy's seat with the reins in one hand, a whip poised in the other; first thought was that the visitor might be Henry Mortonson himself, come to discuss her husband's estate with Susan Telford.

But that couldn't be it—he didn't fill enough of the seat to be the portly banker. Puzzled, Wheelock could only stand motionless and wait as the buggy came rolling into the yard, to a stop near the house. The sorrel tossed its head at the pull of the reins. Now a foot in an elegantly polished high-but-toned shoe emerged, groping for the stepiron; a narrow-hipped figure in a brown suit backed its way

188

out of the rig and stepped down to earth—a figure in a tight, high collar and a bowler hat.

Burn Wheelock's head jerked up as he saw it was Walter Allen's clerk, Ned Hershel, dressed in his Sunday best—at which Wheelock remembered suddenly that this *was* Sunday, and therefore the fellow's day off. Two days after the funeral, it looked as though he had come calling on Rebecca Savage in a rented livery stable rig!

And here was Rebecca, stepping outside with an arm raised to shield her eyes as she identified the visitor. Standing there in the sun, wearing a frilly yellow summer dress, she exclaimed in surprise and Wheelock thought he could hear the pleasure in her voice. 'Why, it's Mr Hershel! How very nice to see you!'

The bowler hat came off. 'How are you, Becky?' Hearing the man use her mother's pet name for her—one he himself hadn't yet had the nerve to attempt—Burn Wheelock clenched his jaws in irritation. 'I took the liberty,' Ned Hershel said, indicating the shining rig and the waiting horse. 'It's such a nice day, I was hoping you might be in the mood to take a little spin.'

'Oh, it's a beautiful day,' she agreed, 'and I'd *love* a ride.' She hesitated, smoothed her skirt with her hands. 'I'll have to change into something more suitable,' she told him, smiling. 'Mama's just finished putting the icing on a chocolate cake. Won't you come in for a slice, and a cup of coffee?'

'Sounds wonderful.' Hershel got out the anchor weight and snapped it to the sorrel's harness. When he joined her on the stoop, Rebecca ushered him inside with a gesture but afterward turned and looked across the yard toward the barn; now she caught up her flounced skirt and started in that direction, and Burn Wheelock quickly bent for the wheelbarrow handles to finished trundling his load down the ramp.

Before he could escape he heard the girl call his name. Caught, he made his face carefully expressionless before he turned. 'Yeah?' he said as gruffly as possible.

She faltered, as though his expression disconcerted her. 'Burn, could you stop long enough to join us for coffee and cake?'

'Me? Do I look like I'm in fit shape to sit down with company?'

Wheelock indicated his clothing, that was rather generously spattered with the results of his labor, but her eyes remained pinned on his face. She looked troubled. Her brow knotted and she exclaimed suddenly, 'Are—are you mad at me about something?'

'Why should I be mad?' he countered, with a shrug. He was damned if he'd let her say anything to make him feel better. 'Well,' he added, 'I better get on with this.' He left her staring after him and headed for the place, some distance behind the barn, where he was

190

dumping his loads. When he returned, with the pitchfork rattling in the empty wheelbarrow, Rebecca had vanished into the house.

And so Burn Wheelock flung himself into his work, in a perfect frenzy of angry energy. He reveled in the injustice of that slick-ear sitting at the table in his Sunday dress-up, being plied with Susan's chocolate cake while Rebecca Savage smiled on him—all without a thought for the lonely exile toiling at his smelly task in the barn. It was anything but fair, and it would serve them right if he simply saddled his crowbait and rode away and left them with it. That would show them! Let 'em find somebody else to do their dirty work!

And then, as he started out on what should be his final trip to the manure pile, he found Ned Hershel waiting in the doorway for him.

The fellow was right in the road and gave no sign of moving out of it, and Wheelock was damned if he would go around. When the manure-spattered wheel nearly touched the man's neatly polished toe, he set the wheelbarrow down and straightened while he demanded coldly, 'Was there something you wanted with me?'

The other took his time, answering. Apparently he had come outside to wait while Rebecca changed for her ride. Now as he eyed Wheelock he produced a box of ready-mades, selected one, and snapped a sulfur alight against the rim of the wheel. As he got his cigarette going, he pointed out, 'You had yourself a good time at my expense, the other day in the store. I just thought I'd like to see how you look in *your* work clothes.' He ran a mocking glance over his rival's spattered garments. '*Cowboy*!' he added with the faintest of sneers, and dropped the burned-out match into the load in the wheelbarrow.

Next moment his shoulders heaved a couple of times within the neat box coat, and his eyes watered slightly as he evidently swallowed some smoke the wrong way.

Burn Wheelock's fists were clenched in the effort to hold his temper. 'You've made your point,' he said finally when he trusted himself. 'I guess we're even.' And he picked up the wheelbarrow by its handles, maneuvering to swing around past his rival.

'I'm not quite finished,' Ned Hershel told him crisply. 'I just don't like the looks of it—you alone, out here, with Becky and her mother. I think you'd better be sure you watch your manners.'

'How about watching your own?' Wheelock snapped back at him. 'On that buggy ride...'

The other turned slowly red. His mouth opened and closed a time or two like the mouth of a fish, and then he drew himself up to full height as he cried, in fierce indignation, 'Are you trying to suggest I might have improper intentions?' It sounded like a speech he'd read in some newspaper serial. Wheelock looked at him a moment, debating whether there was any point in answering. He finally decided against it, and moved again to trundle his load on by.

'Sir! I'm talking to you!'

'You sure are!' Wheelock growled in passing. 'Only, I got something more important here that craves my attention.'

Hershel gasped. Next moment he had tossed aside his cigarette and was stripping out of his coat, revealing a candy-striped shirt and fancy sleeve guards. He carefully folded the coat and laid it on a handy crate, placing his bowler on top of it. That done, he hitched up his pants, spat on his hands, and went running after Wheelock who had deliberately moved on, paying him no heed. Ned Hershel got around in front of the wheelbarrow and set himself in a crouch with back arched and shoulders squared, both fists cocked and ready—the classic fighter's pose. 'All right, mister!' he cried, in a voice that shook with his excitement. 'I think I'm going to have to teach you some manners!'

Wheelock eyed him up and down. 'I just don't think I'd care to learn 'em from you,' he answered.

'Afraid?' the other cried. With the toe of one high-but-toned shoe he drew a long line in the dirt, after which he dropped again into his rigid stance. 'Just step across that! I dare you!'

Burn Wheelock looked at the line. It was drawn in such fashion that, whether he wanted to fight or not, there was no way he could continue with his business without stepping over it. And so, seeing he had no choice, he sighed and deliberately pushed his load across.

Hershel gave a shout of triumph, 'Ah-*hah*!' and at once began ducking and weaving and dancing about in a way that started the dust boiling up around him in a yellow cloud. His rival, who so far hadn't so much as lifted a hand, stared in astonishment at his footwork, and at the left fist held cocked against his chest while the right jabbed quick tattoos at empty air.

With it all, the fellow kept a safe distance and not a blow came near to landing. Finally tiring of the exhibition, Wheelock grunted, 'This is just dumb!' He leaned for the wheelbarrow's handles. But that put his jaw forward, unprotected, and without warning Ned Hershel hit him on it.

Surprised, mainly, he staggered back a couple of paces. Landing a shot even by accident seemed to startle all the boxing science out of his opponent. Hershel came charging, flailing wild blows that did no damage but kept the other busy warding them off with forearms and elbows. All the same, Wheelock couldn't find it amusing—his jaw had started to ache and he was rapidly losing his temper. When Ned Hershel suddenly caught him in the ribs with one of those wild ones, Wheelock swore and, thoroughly angry, poked past his defenses and pasted him solidly in the nose.

A flood of crimson gushed forth. Set back on his heels for only an instant, Hershel swore and ducked his head and came floundering in again; at the same moment, from near at hand came a shocked cry, in Rebecca Savage's voice: 'Burn Wheelock! *Stop* this! Do you hear me?'

He was too busy to answer. All he wanted to do, himself, was put an end to the thing, and when he saw his chance he didn't hold anything back. He threw a punch, and felt the pain of it clear to his shoulder as his knuckles made solid connection against Hershel's round skull. The blow landed just right. It flung the young man clear around, blood from his nose flying. His feet tangled. He stumbled against the wheelbarrow and flopped, belly down, across it; the wheelbarrow went over under him and dumped its load, with Ned Hershel gasping at the bottom.

'Burn!'

He hadn't seen the girl arrive. She stood with one hand clutching her skirt, the other pressed to a cheek that had gone chalk white. She was staring at Wheelock, in horror.

'Well—I stopped it!' he muttered as he backed away from his fallen opponent, shaking his right arm to get some feeling into it.

'But, to fight with a *guest* . . .'

'*I* never invited him!'

Ned Hershel sat up. Apparently dazed, he looked around and then down at himself, and seemed to register what had happened to him. Rebecca asked anxiously, 'Ned, are you all right? Here—let me help you!'

'No! No!' He shook his head vigorously. 'I'm not fit to be touched!' Evading her hand, he took hold of the overturned wheelbarrow and so climbed to his feet. He passed a shirt sleeve across his mouth and stared at the blood that came away on it.

'Oh! This is dreadful!' the girl exclaimed, almost in tears. 'Let me have your shirt, and I'll wash it for you...'

'The shirt is the least of it.' Gingerly he brushed at himself, leaned down and took each pants leg in turn and shook it. When he straightened again he said woodenly, 'I think I'd better go now. Perhaps we can take that ride another time. Please thank your mother for the cake.'

She nodded wordlessly. Hershel refused even to look at Wheelock. He went and got his hat and coat off the box where he had placed them, and then he walked stiffly toward his waiting rig, his whole body tense with outrage. And Rebecca, with a last reproachful glance at Wheelock, followed anxiously after him.

*   *   *

In a prodigious frenzy of activity, by suppertime when he knocked off Burn Wheelock had done almost two full days' work in the barn and had temporary night quarters set up for himself. He washed up in a bucketful of water he'd toted from the creek, traded his soiled and sweated clothing for the new ones he'd bought in town. He combed his hair into shape with his fingers, and then seated himself on a box and sourly contemplated the results of his labor while he built a cigarette.

He had a match poised to snap alight on a thumbnail when he heard Susan, at the house, calling him to supper. He hesitated, then deliberately popped the sulfur in a spurt of flame and took his time getting the cigarette to burning. He tossed the dead match aside and settled back with his smoke.

Minutes later, another call—Rebecca's voice, this time—came across the yard: 'Burn, didn't you hear? Supper's on.' He scowled and made no move to answer. He stayed where he was, and through the barn's wide doors watched the golden afterglow of sunset turn grainy, then thin to early dusk. By now there was a semicircle of burned-down quirly butts in the straw litter at his feet. Suddenly, with a convulsive movement, Burn Wheelock plucked the last one from his lips.

'You know what you're doing, don't you?' he said aloud.

'You're acting like a spoiled brat! Sooner or later, you know you're gonna have to apologize.' He gave a groan, dropped the cigarette and ground it savagely under one boot toe. He got to his feet, gave his pants a hitch. 'This ain't going to be easy,' he warned himself.

He made himself walk out of the barn.

Lamplight bloomed, yellow and friendly, in the windows of the house yonder, and he saw someone move across the kitchen window—Susan, he thought, clearing away the evening meal that he'd stubbornly insisted on missing. Well, he might as well go over and face the music. He crossed the darkening yard; approaching the door, he wondered if he should just enter as though nothing had happened, or whether, under the circumstances, it wouldn't be a better idea to knock and ask if it was all right.

And then, when he was almost at the steps, he saw a movement in the dark and realized someone was seated there. When he realized it was Rebecca, indecision halted him in his tracks. His tongue seemed fastened to his palate.

Her voice emerged from the shadows; it sounded faintly quavering and unsure. 'Burn?' He mumbled something and she went on, 'I—I almost came out to the barn. I want to talk to you.'

'I guess that makes two of us,' he answered gruffly.

'Will you sit down a moment?' Wheelock hesitated but she was already making room on the step beside her. Gingerly he took his place.

198

There was an awkward silence while he tried to gather his resources; then apparently both had an impulse to speak, at the same instant. Their words collided and fell of their own weight.

Rebecca placed a hand on Wheelock's and her fingers felt cold. 'Look!' she exclaimed. 'Before you say a word. Let me say I—I'm sorry for how I talked to you.'

Wheelock turned his head to stare, but could make out no more than the pale outline of her face. 'You're sorry?' he blurted. 'Then—you ain't mad? I was sure you held me to blame for the fight,' he went on uncertainly. 'Hershel was the one that insisted on one. I couldn't talk him out of it. Honest! That's the truth!'

'But I don't understand why he would do such a thing.'

'Well—' He could have lied. Instead, however reluctantly, he admitted, 'I guess I can't honestly say but what he had some excuse. The other day, in town, I sort of got off on the wrong foot with him— and all my fault. I couldn't help it! There's just something about that gent—'

'I know,' Rebecca agreed with a sigh. 'He *is* an awful stuffed shirt, isn't he? But he was kind to Mama,' she went on, with Wheelock hardly believing his ears. 'Taking care of the funeral for us, and all. I feel we just *have* to be nice to him.'

He drew a long breath, that was shaky with relief. 'I guess I thought it might be something more than that. I was beginning to be afraid you *liked* him!'

She hesitated, '"Afraid," Burn?' she echoed then, an odd note in her voice. 'But—why on earth would that bother you?'

'I know—it wouldn't really have been none of my business. Trouble is, it's like I feel everything about you has become my business!'

There was a pause, during which the voice of the creek from beyond the house seemed to fill the dusk around them. He was aware of the girl staring at him, her eyes probing his dimly visible features. Finally she said, in a small voice, 'What are you trying to tell me, Burn?'

He shrugged. 'That I'm nutty about you, I guess. And there ain't no telling what a man will do when he's jealous! Maybe get in a fight, for no reason at all. Like Ned Hershel—I kind of think he's got the same problem.'

'Jealous of *me*?'

'I know. It's dumb to blurt out a thing like that. But, I figure you got a right to understand what happened today—and why I been acting like a kicked dog, just because you saw fit to bawl me out a little.'

Suddenly she was on her feet, moving away from him. Burn Wheelock stumbled up hastily. He didn't dare to touch her; he spoke earnestly to her back, trying clumsily to make amends for his foolishness. 'Look! I never meant to upset you with such talk. I won't do it again.

200

'I always been pretty pleased with myself,' he plunged ahead, when she made no answer. 'Plumb satisfied to draw good pay as a top buckaroo—ram around and see a lot of country, nothing on my mind to speak of besides my hat.

'But suddenly everything's different. I'm thinking about a talk I had with a rancher up at Antelope—an old German fellow, named Fred Adler; I know, now, he made a lot of sense. He tried to warn me. He said, one of these times, something could happen to change my mind about how good things look, the other side of the next hill. Well, it appears to of happened. You don't need to worry, though,' he insisted miscrably. 'I won't make a pest of myself about it. Never even meant you should know. It just slipped out.'

He paused for breath. When she still didn't say anything, he added gruffly, 'Well, I got my chores to do. I'll see you in the morning.'

He had taken only a couple of steps when she stopped him; her voice sounded rather strange. 'Wait!' Wheelock half turned. In the light from the window he could see her faintly, one hand half raised. As he looked at her, wondering and hopeful, she dropped the hand and said, 'You—you didn't have any dinner.'

'Ain't much hungry,' he told her. 'I'll make up for it at breakfast.' And he turned away and left her standing there.

CHAPTER FIFTEEN

Jess Croy had managed to make short work of his inspection trip to the Upper Deschutes. He saw it as no more than an excuse, thought up by Youngdahl to get him out of sight long enough for the fuss over Rufe Flagg to simmer down; it wasn't worth spending any more time in the saddle than was absolutely necessary.

And he played in luck. Just south of Farewell Bend on the Deschutes, he ran across a rancher he knew who was in process of pushing a jag of stock up into the high country of the Cascades. Croy shared a noon camp with the outfit, passing around coffee and grub and a bottle from somebody's saddle pocket, while the boss filled him in on conditions in his region after the preceding tough winter. They were bad enough, as Croy could have predicted, and there wasn't much likelihood of Youngdahl finding much stock for sale there; presumably he'd have to look over in Idaho, or Nevada. And so, satisfied that he had learned all he needed, Croy went no farther with his quest but turned off instead across the juniper desert, the thirty miles east toward Prineville.

Youngdahl had allowed him two weeks and he meant to make the most of them. With almost five days to kill before he had to report back to work, he rode into the village at noon of a summer day when Main Street lay quiet and almost empty. At such a moment Prineville might look dead enough; but the place had saloons and restaurants and a cat house, and Jess Croy looked forward confidently to enjoying himself.

This mood lasted as long as it took him to dismount in front of Haze's.

He was tying to the hitchrail when someone stepped out through the open doorway; he took an incurious look and froze in his tracks as he recognized Sam Rankin. The sheriff of Wasco County was the last man Croy would have expected or wanted to see, here so far from his own bailiwick. With enough presence of mind to take a sidling step and put the horse between them, Croy ducked as though to inspect a pastern in the moment that Rankin's head turned in his direction.

He waited out a bad moment, expecting to hear himself hailed and confronted. When he finally risked a glance under the horse's neck, he saw to his relief that Rankin was already moving off up the street. Croy narrowly watched him go, rubbing a palm across his heavy mustache; afterward he cast a speculative glance toward the door of the saloon and, with curiosity gnawing at him, walked around his tied horse and inside.

There were no customers; the big, low-ceilinged room held a kind of smothering stillness. Behind the bar, Gil Haze had just finished filling and trimming a kerosene lamp. He turned and placed it on a shelf and nodded brief greeting. 'Haven't seen you down this way for a spell,' he commented.

'No,' Jess Croy agreed. He added: 'What was Sam Rankin doing?'

'Having a beer,' the saloonkeeper said, and picked up the empty glass where it sat in a ring of spilled suds.

'Hell! I mean, what's he doing in Prineville? This ain't his county.'

Before answering, Haze deposited the beer glass in a wreck pan beneath the bar, and started mopping up the wooden counter with a rag. 'He come in on the stage yesterday evening, told me he was looking for Sheriff Blake on some business or other. But Jim must be out of town, because this morning Rankin still hadn't been able to find him.'

'He didn't happen to say what his business was?'

Croy tried to make the question sound casual, but he knew from the sharp look he got that the other wasn't taken in. Haze told him bluntly, 'His business had to deal with the law—which means I couldn't discuss it over the bar, even if I happened to know.' He gave that a moment to sink in, and then pointedly asked, 'You drinking?'

Jess Croy stared at him balefully, feeling the angry heat rise through his cheeks. 'Later!' he said curtly, and turned and strode out of there.

Standing in front of the saloon, he scouted the street in search of Rankin, but failed to see him. He scowled as he asked himself if this meant he was going to have to forgo the holiday he'd planned on. With Sam Rankin here in Prineville—for whatever reason—there was too much risk of running into him; and Croy could admit to himself, if not to anyone else, that the tough sheriff had a way of making him uneasy.

After all, he didn't know what had been going on in his absence. Rankin might even have got his hands on that sonofabitch Wheelock, and dragged from him the full story of Rufe Flagg's hanging; in which case—and that was the frightening thing—Jess Croy could be in real trouble and not even aware of it...

Just then he saw Rankin, on a black horse, riding out of the wide entrance of Hamilton's Livery in the next block. With a quick instinct to hide, Croy drew back into the protection of a beer shield fastened up beside Haze's doorway, but Rankin had already turned north. Croy stood and watched him ride away, lifting the black into a lope and stitching a rhythm of hoofbeats across the village quiet. Steel shoes thudded briefly on the plank bridge across Ochoco Creek. Then the sheriff was gone, and the way of his going suggested he had settled down to a purposeful mission.

Jess Croy thought about this for a moment;

then he went out and mounted his own animal, freeing the reins from the tie pole with a savage jerk. He rode across the intersection, past the big box of a hotel on the corner, and dismounted in front of Hamilton's where he walked up the ramp and into the musty interior.

A man was emptying bags of oats into a bin, toward the rear; grain dust hung about him in a fog and the noise he made covered Croy's approach, so that when he spoke the hostler gave a start and whirled letting oats spray out over the splintered floor.

'What the hell!' he blurted.

'You know me?' Jess Croy demanded.

The hostler looked at him blankly. 'I don't reckon.'

'What about the man that just left here? Did you know *him*?'

'Sure. That was the Wasco County sheriff.'

'And he got a horse from you?'

The man nodded, his black eyes unreadable. 'Wanted it for day hire.'

Croy asked, 'Where was he going?'

At that the other hesitated, slowly wiping his hands on the legs of his overalls. 'I just ain't sure it concerns you, mister.'

'Nobody said it did. But I'm curious—and when my curiosity ain't satisfied, I can be a lot mean!' Suddenly Jess Croy reached and gathered the front of the overalls in one hand, deliberately twisting it so that the hostler was

206

drawn up onto the toes of his heavy work shoes. Croy held him like that a moment, close enough that, even in this half-darkness, he could see a trace of sweat that broke out along the plane of one cheek. Just as deliberately, Croy released him.

'Now,' he suggested. 'Suppose you tell me exactly what the sheriff said.'

The other swallowed, and when he spoke his voice held a tremor. 'He wanted to know how to get to the Telford place. It's north of town, ten miles on the main wagon road—'

Croy cut him off. 'What did he want to know for?'

'I had an idea he was interested in a new fellow they got working there. Young guy with a funny name: Whitlock? No! Wheelock— that's it . . .'

Croy stared; it was as though something lurched and turned over deep inside him. It was only when he became aware of curiosity beginning to replace fear in the hostler's expression, that he managed to shrug and say roughly, 'Well, that's all right. For a minute, there, I thought a friend of mine might have got himself in trouble of some kind. And of course, that's crazy, because Sam Rankin ain't got authority this side of the Wasco County line.'

'They bend those lines sometimes,' the other suggested helpfully.

Jess Croy nearly hit him for bringing that up. Even as it was, the look on his face must have been startling because the man backed away a step, until the open grain bin pressed against the backs of his legs. He looked only a little relieved when Croy muttered, 'If it ain't my friend the sheriff's after, then I don't give a good damn what he does.'

But Croy's face was set and grim, belieing his words, as he turned his back and left the fellow standing there.

In sunshine again, blinking a little after the barn's shadows, he whipped the reins free and lifted into the saddle. When he rode, northward across the bridge and along the wagon road toward the wall that rimmed the canyon, he almost thought he could smell the acrid dust settling behind the passage of Sam Rankin, short minutes ahead of him.

*   *   *

Burn Wheelock had left the ranch that morning forking one of the wagon team horses that had been broken more or less to a saddle, and carrying his day's rations in saddlebags he'd found in the barn. Things were pretty much at a standstill. With no word yet from the banker, and having mended everything in sight around headquarters, he was restless for some sort of activity.

So he told the women he wanted a look at the hill country and water sources adjacent to Reub Telford's deeded holdings, to make an

208

estimate of the number of cattle they could run on summer range when funds for stocking the ranch became available. Actually this was a task that could well have used two or three days of riding; but, aware of Susan's uneasiness over being left without a man on the place, he planned to cut his inspection short and be back by nightfall.

Morning sun was drawing mist off the hills in smoking streamers. It felt good to be in the saddle again, using different muscles and engaged in something other than menial repair jobs with ax and hammer. He enjoyed himself, while busily recording everything he saw on a mental map where, in the fashion of an outdoorsman, he would keep it forever afterward fixed, landmarks and distances and directions indelibly set.

He was generally well satisfied. The shape of the hills limited the amount of summer range available, but at the same time the number of cattle outfits that might have to compete for it would be determined by the narrowness of the McKay Creek canyon, below. He could see this grass had been used to some extent, probably by Reub Telford, but not on any scale.

Though the Telford ranch would always be a small outfit, he was sure it could be made to pay.

When he judged from the sun it was time he turned back, Wheelock first had a leisurely meal from his saddle supplies. The sandwiches had been put up for him by Rebecca, and as he ate his thoughts turned to her—as they usually did, when he had a few moments to himself. Since that evening on the steps, however, he had pretty much kept away from her. What he had said and done that night embarrassed him; he was bound not to cause her any more painful moments, just because he happened to be a damn fool.

At least, he reminded himself as he got back into the saddle, she was still speaking to him. It was as much as he had any right to hope for, after what he'd done, and he was grateful...

In his hours of riding today he had been whistled at by a marmot and once had sent a Steller's jay screaming away, startled, across the sunlit timber; otherwise he'd had the silences to himself and seen hardly a living thing. He had so got into thinking he was alone that for a moment it failed to shock through to him when, rounding a tree-capped shoulder of lava rock, he all at once found himself sitting face to face with Sam Rankin.

He was the last person Burn Wheelock would have expected, and his mind emptied with the shock. The Wasco County sheriff had pulled up his own horse and now sat waiting, obviously, for the other man to come to him; drawing rein at a distance of a dozen feet, Wheelock stared back without speaking. Rankin, he saw, was not wearing his sheriff's star openly, nor had he made a move to pull the

210

gun from his holster; but Wheelock's weapon was in a saddle pocket, completely out of reach.

For just an instant he considered yanking the reins and turning his horse, thinking he might regain the point of rocks he'd passed a moment ago. He actually lifted the reins, but it was a hopeless maneuver and Rankin, plainly reading the desperate thought in his face, shook his narrow head and spoke a mild warning. 'No, Wheelock. Don't try it.'

So he forced himself to relax, but the muscles of his cheeks and jaw were drawn tight; his face felt like a mask. 'Supposing I had?' he said, and had to keep his voice from shaking.

'I told you, back in Antelope,' the sheriff said, 'if you ran out on me I'd take it as an admission of guilt and I'd bring you back. Maybe you didn't figure I meant it.'

'I didn't figure to see you *here*. You're way out of your territory.'

'Did you think that would stop me?'

Wheelock shook his head. 'Not you,' he admitted bitterly. He added: 'Maybe you'll tell me how you ran me down?'

'It's never as hard, as the man you're after seems to think,' Rankin assured him. 'A matter mostly of asking questions in the right places. Of course, sometimes they don't want to answer your questions at first—like that pair of ladies at the ranch house.'

Stiffening, Wheelock snapped, 'You were

211

down there? Making trouble for them?'

'No trouble. I don't work that way. Still, they seemed disinclined to talk to me at all once they found out who I was looking for. They argued it betwixt themselves, and I noticed the older one kept looking off this direction as though she was afraid you'd ride up any minute. It finally gave me the idea that if I did some circling around, I just might pick up sign on you. So I thanked them and left.'

'Looks like you managed!'

The sheriff nodded. 'I never was too much at reading trail—you lost me good, that day on Antelope Creek. But, this time I ran in luck.'

A cloud crossed the sun, like the working of a camera's shutter; the light dimmed and then brightened again around them. Wheelock's horse dipped its head and he almost unconsciously gave it rein length so it could pull at a clump of bunch grass.

Wheelock filled his lungs. 'Did you tell the women why you wanted me?' he demanded harshly.

'Never told them anything. The regard those two have for you,' Rankin said, and a knowing tilt quirked his thin lips, 'I judged it would be a mistake to let on I was the law. Whatever they might know, *you've* told them. I guess at that, you must have done some talking, because that young one—quite a looker, ain't she?—well, can you imagine? She even asked if my name was Flagg!

'Just lucky for her it was a wrong guess!' the sheriff added dryly. 'The two of them seemed to be alone there. And maybe you ain't aware of this, Wheelock, but it's pretty damned certain the Flaggs ride these hills, on occasion. If they *were* to come on a couple of unprotected women, on a ranch as remote as that one—you might not want to study on what could happen!'

It caused a tightening in the gut, hearing this man voice a fear that had troubled him often enough. Wheelock demanded sharply, 'What would bring the Flaggs to McKay Creek?'

Rankin shrugged. 'We can't prove it yet, but there ain't much doubt they deal in stolen stock that they pick up wherever they find it. And it's equally clear in *my* mind—even if I can't prove that, either—that they must have connections here in the Ochocos, probably more than one fence acting as outlets for what they steal. Instead of trying to deal with big herds, it's my view they split the stuff up and work it off in small bunches, which makes it harder to trace.

'I'm willing to bet the Vigilante crowd that used to run Crook County probably knew all about what was going on, maybe took a cut. The new sheriff, Jim Blake, is honest but he hasn't been in office long enough to get matters in hand. But, by God! Someday, we'll nail that crew!'

'Seems to me,' Wheelock pointed out bitterly, 'you're going to a helluva lot of trouble to punish the men you think may be guilty of hanging one of them!'

That obviously stung. The narrow face tinged with color. Rankin's mouth hardened and he said flatly, 'I'm not arguing the point with you again! Murder is murder—whoever does it and whoever it's done to. Right now, I'll thank you to get your hands up, mister!'

As he spoke, an unhurried movement pushed back the skirt of his coat and then a long-barreled Colt was in his grasp, pointed at Wheelock. The latter hesitated only a moment, eying the gun and the implacable face of the one who held it. Resignedly he lifted his empty hands.

Rankin kneed the black and walked it toward him, the gun's muzzle never wavering. Pulling in alongside Wheelock's animal, he reached and flipped back the front of the prisoner's jacket. 'Where's your gun?' he demanded. 'I know you've got one.'

'In the saddle pocket,' Wheelock told him, seeing nothing to gain by a lie. 'That one.' He indicated it with a jerk of the head. Sam Rankin moved his horse a step nearer, and leaned to undo the fastenings and lift the leather flap.

As close to Wheelock as that, the man's tawny eyes suddenly widened, the narrow face went slack. His whole body loosened; he started to spill forward, then, falling limply against Burn Wheelock as echoes of a rifle went

214

booming and breaking along the timbered ridges.

CHAPTER SIXTEEN

The apple pie Susan had just taken from the oven and set out on the table to cool filled the kitchen with its pleasant, sweet-and-spice aroma. Rebecca, washing dishes at the sink, heard her mother's chatter without actually being aware of it; she was too much concerned over the stranger who had come asking for Burn Wheelock.

The sharp, ruddy face, the bitter mouth and fanatic intensity of the eyes had bothered her more than the man's probing questions. She was sure, even in the moment she suggested it, that he couldn't possibly be part of the family Burn had said were looking for him—he wasn't big enough, hard enough; he didn't have the manner of a hillbilly. Yet she had known he spelled danger. Whatever he may have wanted, something told her he wasn't one to be put off easily. Her thoughts kept frantically circling the question of somehow letting Burn Wheelock know, of getting a warning to him. But all too obviously, there simply was no way...

She was deep in these thoughts, and the touch of Susan's hand on her arm startled her.

Rebecca looked at her mother, saw her head tilted to one side and a finger lifted for attention. Frowning, Susan repeated, 'Be still a moment!' And then, 'What do I hear?'

With the clatter of pans quieted, Rebecca listened and now she heard it too. 'Somebody's moving cattle. Up on the road . . .'

The bawling in protesting throats seemed to grow louder, now that they were aware of it. 'It's getting nearer,' Susan murmured, and hurried off to a window that would give her a view of the road, and of the plank bridge over McKay Creek. 'Oh, my goodness!' she cried. '*Look!*'

Rebecca hastily wiped her hands, and went to join her.

There were twenty-five or thirty head, of mixed breeds and sizes. Four riders were working them, holding them bunched with shouts and flapping coils of rope; and now, as the women watched, the cattle were being turned off the road and pushed straight across the creek toward the ranchyard. Some took the bridge; the rest crowded into the water, bellowing, to paw and scramble their way up the nearer bank. 'What do those men think they're doing?' Susan exclaimed. 'They've got no business here! Can't they see this is private property?'

Rebecca was whipping off her apron. 'I intend to tell them!' she said grimly.

By the time she reached the door and was

down the steps, her mother close behind, the last of the beef was across and plodding past the buildings. Dust rose, lowered heads swayed, horns flashed. They were being pointed, obviously, for the lower meadow. And now one of the yelling riders saw the women and, peeling off from the drive, came spurring over.

He was a big fellow, astride a blue roan horse whose flanks, still dripping from the creek, bore the bloody marks of the rowels. He pulled in so sharply his animal was sent back on its haunches. Pale eyes peered from a mean face, that showed reddish glints of unshaven whiskers. 'Where's Reub?' he demanded without preamble. 'We brought some stuff for him.'

The abrupt question jarred an answer out of Susan. 'But—my husband's dead.'

'Dead!' the man echoed. 'The hell he is! Since when?'

'Last week.' Her voice faltered under the stab of those piercing, protuberant eyes. 'There was an accident.'

'The hell!' he repeated, as though he only half believed her. A second rider was approaching. This was an older man; gray hair, that had a greasy look to it, whipped about his face as he closed the distance. The younger one didn't wait but called out, 'Pa! They say Telford's gone and died on us since we was here last.'

Big as he was, his father looked even bigger. He rode a tough gray horse that fidgeted around under him when he had reined in. He pushed back a shapeless hat and Rebecca saw with a shudder that his eyes were ill matched, each showing a lot of white in turn as they shifted their focus on her. Like his son, he was roughly dressed and wore a revolver strapped to his waist. A battered-looking rifle stock thrust from the saddle scabbard under his knee.

The younger one said, 'Pa, does this mean we got to take this beef elsewhere?'

A sharp, slicing motion with one liver-spotted hand waved him to silence. 'We'll see— we'll see.' The mismated eyes raked the women again, as they stood with the horses looming before them. 'Who are you two?' he demanded in his highpitched, grating voice. 'I never seen either of you.'

Susan's voice faltered slightly but she managed to answer. 'I'm Mrs Reuben Telford. This is my daughter.'

'Oh?' Gray-stubbled cheeks stirred, as the old man worked at the chewing tobacco he kept tucked into one of them. 'Who else you got staying with you?'

Suddenly afraid to hear her mother's answer, Rebecca blurted hastily, 'There's nobody. We're all alone here.' And then felt her knees shake as she saw the younger one peer at her with keener, almost wolfish interest.

His father showed no expression at all. 'You're lying,' he said abruptly. The wave of a hand indicated the buildings around them. 'Somebody's put a lot of sweat into this place, recent. Wasn't work the likes of you two could have handled—and if I knew Reub Telford, he'd as soon left it fall down around his ears. So the question is, who was it? And why ain't you wantin' to tell me?' Lank gray hair brushed his shoulders as he turned to his son. 'Homer, you get down and take a look in the house. But be careful—no telling who they might have hiding in there.'

'Sure, Pa.' He took his eyes from Rebecca long enough to lift a cowhide boot across the saddle and step down, dropping the reins to anchor them. Rebecca and Susan drew back as he approached the steps, but they caught the rank animal smell of him, and the sourness of whiskey; he grinned, seeing their reaction. He pulled his gun and, holding it ready, yanked the screen door wide and stepped through it in a single swift movement.

The old man waited with head cocked to one side, listening. The cattle, meanwhile, had been moved onto the meadow and now the two remaining riders, both with the same general appearance of Homer and his father, were coming up at a lope. Rebecca shared a look with Susan, saw her frightened pallor and wished desperately for a chance to say, *You know who these men are, don't you? And why we*

219

can't possibly let them know about Burn Wheelock!

Had there been any doubt, it was settled for her when the blue roan eased around and she saw the Star brand on its bloodied flank...

Homer Flagg reappeared in the doorway. In one fist he held a good quarter of Susan's fresh apple pie. 'Nobody there, Pa,' he announced. 'And nothin' but woman things.'

'The barn, then,' the old man grunted. 'Maybe that's where he stays. Go check it out.'

'Right.'

Homer wolfed the rest of the pie, licked at the juice that had dribbled down his wrist. He wiped his fingers on his shirt and was walking out to the roan when his name was suddenly shouted, from the direction of the corral. One of his kinsmen had paused there and was standing in the stirrups, hands cupped about his mouth as he yelled excitedly: 'Homer! Hey, look here! It's your bronc—the dun that Wheelock bastard got away on, the night he killed Chet...'

Homer Flagg swore, swung into the leather and gave the roan a kick. His father watched him go, no expression at all on that mean and ravaged face; for her part, Rebecca could only wait with sinking spirits while Homer had his look at the dun.

A moment later he came pounding back across the yard with the other pair in his wake. The old man demanded sharply, 'Well? Is it?'

Homer nodded, scowling and grim. And then everything hung fire as the chief of the clan slowly swung his head and laid a long, speculative regard on the silent women.

Deliberately, Noah Flagg tossed his reins to one of his sons, dismounted. He singled out Rebecca and came at a prowl, lithe and loose-hung as a mountain cat, to stand tall and dangerous above her. Somehow she forced herself to meet that wall-eyed stare, though her head was tilted back until she could feel the pulse throbbing in her throat.

He said, in a voice that was almost gentle, 'All right. Now suppose you tell us about that Wheelock fellow.'

She had to swallow before she could speak. 'I don't know anything. That horse wandered in a few days ago. I caught him and put him in the corral...'

The eyes didn't change—the left one burning into her own, while the right seemed to be gazing off somewhere past her shoulder. But now one big hand came up and the heavy fingers spread across her face. They smelled of tobacco and gun oil and horse sweat. The rope-hardened palm clamped down on her jaw and the fingers tightened, squeezing; the agony of muscle grinding against her cheekbones suddenly made her knees sag and she thought she could not endure it another moment without crying out.

The fingers eased off, just a trifle, but

221

without releasing their grip. 'Try again,' Noah Flagg suggested. 'And make it the truth this time. Tell me about Burn Wheelock...'

*   *   *

In the moment following the rifle shot, though he heard it clearly and saw Sam Rankin's alarming behavior, Burn Wheelock couldn't really believe what had happened. The sheriff, staring straight into his eyes as he leaned toward him from the saddle, looked like a man about to speak and make some statement in confidence. Wheelock simply waited—and then, in amazement, he saw the expression run out of the narrow, ruddy features, and his own shocked senses registered that something was wrong. Almost too late he had presence of mind to put out his hands, trying to catch the other's weight as it came slacking against him.

The rifle spoke again.

It had the range. A slug bounced off an outthrust of lava in front of Wheelock's horse, with a sound like the whine of a hornet; and the animal went crazy in a pinwheel turn that spun it clear around. Wheelock's hands were torn loose from their attempt to hold Rankin in the saddle. He had a glimpse of the sheriff's gun spinning out of his grasp in a smear of sunlight, of Rankin himself disappearing in a limp, groundward sprawl. Then the antics of the horse threw him off balance and he felt the saddle go from under him; he lost one stirrup, kicked wildly free of the other to keep from being dragged. He fell, and hit the earth solidly, and a steel-shod hoof knocked the hat from his head and just missed taking his brains with it.

Stunned, most of the breath knocked out of him, he couldn't possibly have moved just then. He lay in a sprawl with a cheek pressed against the dirt, and watched a beetle scramble over a clump of grass within inches of his nose. There was little sound—a muted wash of wind through trees on the ridge above him and, carried to his ear along the sounding board of the earth, an occasional ripping noise. Some part of his brain identified that as made by one of the horses, that had stopped some little distance away and was pulling at the grass.

Burn Wheelock felt terribly exposed, lying here with the sun warm upon his back. He was out in the open, too far from any rock or log or even any slight declivity that might give him protection. He could imagine the rifle muzzle that might even now be trained on him, the eyes that could be studying him and trying to decide whether he was dead or not. He concentrated on looking as dead as possible, while he sought to make some kind of sense of what was happening.

His first thought, after that talk with the sheriff, was of the Flaggs—the moment of violence had been incredibly brief, the shots so confusingly blended that he couldn't have

223

sworn they both came from the same weapon. Whoever it was up there, or however many, they were bound to want to check on their marksmanship. Yet time continued to drag out, with no break in the stillness; and when the burden of waiting became too great he risked raising his head slightly, turning it just enough so he could peer through the fringe of grass that screened his vision.

Yonder were the two horses, halted by trailing reins and feeding with insolent unconcern for the fate of their riders. There was Rankin, looking like a motionless heap of old clothing. And, some dozen feet away, a stabbing point of brightness that must be sunlight bouncing off Rankin's lost six-shooter, lying there in the dirt.

Wheelock was studying that, estimating the chances of reaching it, when movement at the edge of the trees caught his attention. He froze, afraid now to move at all.

A man had emerged from the timber at the foot of the ridge, leading a horse. Leaf shadows filtered over him deceptively while Wheelock peered through squinted eyes, and felt the wild thudding of his heart as he lay on it. He saw the rifle, held by the action and swung at arm's length. And then he saw the man's face.

It was Jess Croy.

Burn Wheelock blinked—Youngdahl's foreman, here in a hidden meadow of the Ochocos, was a possibility that had never entered his mind. But Croy's intentions were clear enough. He paused, looked long at the crumpled figure of Sam Rankin, then swung his head to peer at Wheelock. After that he came on, the horse bobbing its head as it plodded after him at the end of the reins. Plainly, the rifle was for finishing the job it had begun, if necessary. Caught in an awkward position, partly raised off the ground, Burn Wheelock could only hold himself motionless while his muscles bound into knots, and he watched Croy striding nearer across the grass.

Then Sam Rankin stirred, and flopped over from his side onto his back.

Croy's head jerked around. He halted in midstride and dropped the reins of the led horse, so he could bring up his rifle in both hands. And, knowing his purpose, Burn Wheelock saw only one desperate chance of forestalling it. All of Croy's attention was on the man he had shot. Almost without thinking, Wheelock swung to his feet; cramped muscles caused him to stumble as he went at a run toward Rankin's fallen revolver.

Croy must have heard, or caught some glimpse from the tail of his eye. He looked about. Wheelock saw the black fury that distorted his face, the convulsive movement as he turned, lifting the rifle. But he was a shade too quick; one boot slipped, in some manner, and threw him an instant off balance.

It was the only break Burn Wheelock got.

225

He made a flat dive for the revolver, hit jarringly, but with outstretched fingers touching the metal. They snatched it up somehow and he was rolling, hearing the angry lash of the rifle and cringing to the expected blow, felt nothing. And then Croy's solid shape was between him and the sky and he poked the gun at it, and found the trigger.

Powder smoke swept across him. When it cleared, leaving him choking and panting a little with fear and exertion, Jess Croy was no longer there.

It was a long minute before Wheelock could move. Necessity pulled him at last to his hands and knees and then to his feet. His legs seemed not to have any stiffness in them, and the sight of Croy lying sprawled in the grass turned him weaker than ever. But he walked over, carrying the gun, to look at the man he'd killed. Croy's eyes were wide and staring sightlessly at the sky. Wheelock, looking at him, felt a brassy taste in his mouth and suddenly found himself swallowing convulsively.

A sound from Sam Rankin brought him out of that. Rankin had found the strength to lever himself up onto one elbow, in spite of the wound that bloodied his shirt. As Wheelock hurried over, the sheriff demanded hoarsely, 'Did you nail the sonofabitch?' Still unable to speak, Wheelock nodded. 'He nailed me pretty good, too.' Rankin tried to move, his face twisted with pain and he dropped upon his

226

back. 'Well, do something, damn you! Can't you see the shape I'm in?'

Wheelock went to his knees, laying aside the gun. Anybody involved in range work learned a certain amount about dealing with the emergencies that arose when men were isolated, in dangerous pursuits and perhaps miles from aid; he'd set broken arms, and once had tended to a friend who'd taken the point of a steer's horn deep in the thigh. But Wheelock had no experience with anything like this wound of Sam Rankin's. Gingerly he laid aside the front of the blood-soaked jacket, fumbled at the shirt buttons and then, with an angry wrench, popped them off so he could uncover what Jess Croy's rifle bullet had done.

The wonder was that it hadn't done for him. From the welter of blood and torn tissue, Wheelock judged that the rifle slug, hitting a rib a glancing blow, had somehow managed to follow it around from back to front, laying open an angry-looking furrow from which the blood flowed copiously. Looking at the damage, he cleared his throat and warned, 'What little I can do is gonna be pretty crude!'

'Well, get on with it!' the other said tightly. His narrow face shone with perspiration. 'Then get me to somebody who does know what he's doing. Maybe, those women down at the ranch house...'

Wheelock thought of Susan, and was doubtful. On the other hand, Rebecca—even if she'd had no experience with things like this—was surely brave enough, and resourceful enough, to cope with it. At the house, too, there would be proper bandaging, hot water, medication. For now, the very most he could hope would be to stem the flow of bleeding.

Lips pulled back in distaste for the job, he made do with what he had handy, ripping up Rankin's shirt and forming a compress to lay over the wound. Needing more cloth, he tore off the tail of his own shirt, afterward using the sheriff's belt to hold all this in place. He had to move Rankin's body to slip the belt up around his ribs, and was surprised at the man's light weight—he was hard, and wirily muscled, but surprisingly slight of build. He gave limply to the handling.

In moving him, Wheelock felt something in the man's coat pocket that gave off a metallic clink. Curious, he dug it out and stared bleakly at a pair of handcuffs, knowing without being told why the sheriff had brought them along: They'd been meant for Burn Wheelock's own wrists! Resentful over the thought of being dragged back to Wasco County in irons—or maybe, what was even worse, being forced to let Rebecca see him that way—he swore a little, and angrily shoved the ugly things back in the pocket where he'd found them. Afterward, still shaky from the emergency job he'd had to perform, Wheelock settled back on his heels and looked at the man's face. Rankin's eyes were closed. He'd blacked out with the pain.

Wheelock wiped a palm across his own sweating cheeks, breathing deeply. But he couldn't afford to rest. Leaving the sheriff, he rose and went to see about getting Jess Croy onto his saddle. He brought Croy's horse over to where he lay, got the dead man under the arms and tried to lift him. It was no use. The body's dead weight was too much for him; he couldn't manage it, and the horse refused to hold still once it caught the scent of blood. Finally Wheelock said, 'The hell with it!' and let Croy sag limply to the ground.

This was using up too much time; he'd have to come back. He tied the horse to a stump to prevent it straying, and returned to Sam Rankin.

The lawman's eyes were open now, but they held a feverish shine and Wheelock doubted that they saw him. Rankin's dry lips moved and the buckaroo realized he was asking for water. Wheelock didn't have any. He looked around a little helplessly, then remembered a seep spring he'd passed, back along the trail a rod or two. He lacked a container; in desperation he grabbed his hat off the ground, where he'd lost it during the action, and vaulted onto his saddle.

When he returned, carefully carrying his hat filled with water, he got down without spilling it and managed to get a little between the hurt man's lips, and then bathed Rankin's feverish flesh. The compress he'd put on the bullet wound, he saw, was already turning red—he hadn't been able to stop the bleeding. Now as the sheriff brought his eyes into focus, Wheelock told him, 'There's no other way. I'm gonna put you on your horse, and somehow you have to stay on long enough to get you down to the ranch. You understand?

'Then, here we go . . .'

If the sheriff had been any more solidly built or any heavier, Wheelock was convinced he never would have got him into the saddle; for all the help Rankin was able to give him, it proved almost as tough as maneuvering Jess Croy's lifeless body. Finally he hooked the lawman's hand about the horn, and got his boot in the stirrup, and from there was able to hoist him up and swing the other leg across. Once in leather Rankin managed to brace himself against the pommel, but handling the reins was clearly beyond him. So Wheelock took them himself and, mounting his own animal, led off at a slow walk while the hurt man swayed, with bobbing head, to every cautious step.

He thought at first they might actually be going to make it. The motion of the horse seemed to rouse the sheriff, so that he got some stiffness into his supporting arms and even managed to lift his head as though he were aware of what was going on. A mile slipped past this way beneath the slow tread of hoofs,

230

and then another, and Wheelock began mentally charting the distance still to be covered and estimating how long, at their painful gait, it would take them.

Then things went wrong.

The hurt man's behavior suddenly turned erratic. He began to grow slack, to sway more dangerously as he obviously lost control. His eyes were closed now, his bitter mouth bracketed by deep lines of pain and effort; and Wheelock, leading by the reins, had to watch him constantly for fear of seeing him slide limply out of the saddle. He considered tying the hurt man's boots to the stirrups and his hands to the saddlehorn, but rejected that—if he lost consciousness and fell against the horn, Rankin could do serious damage to his bullet wound.

Burn Wheelock was sweating over the problem. He reined in, finally—and just in time, for at that moment all resistance seemed to go out of Rankin's body and he started to fall limply sideward, almost eluding the hand with which Wheelock grabbed his clothing. It cost an effort but Wheelock held him balanced there, long enough that he was able to get down from his own horse and then, carefully, ease the unconscious man to the ground.

Swearing, he looked around him while he tried to figure what to do now.

It was ironic that they had come this far. The hills were mostly behind them, with only a couple of miles to the level canyon floor. Just at this point they were in a gentle flat, rimmed with pine. Someone—not Reub Telford, he was willing to wager—had at one time been working here, probably with the intention of putting up a holding corral: several lodgepoles had been felled and piled handy for the purpose, but nothing more had been done and the timbers were turning gray with weather.

Then Wheelock looked at the ground and could still see, just faintly, the indentations of a wagon's wheels; and that gave him his idea. Where one wagon had gone, so could another. Instantly he returned to the hurt man, knelt and laid a hand on the sheriff's shoulder. 'I'm gonna fetch a rig,' he said, speaking slowly and distinctly. 'To haul you down—it's the only thing I can think of. Do you hear me?'

There was no response at all. But Rankin's chest rose and fell evenly to his breathing, and Wheelock could detect a strong pulsebeat in his throat. He looked at the wound, and though he could not be certain he rather imagined the bleeding had stopped—he let himself believe it. Decision made, he took the sheriff under the arms and hauled him into a pine tree's shade, where he tried to make him comfortable. He tied the man's horse to a limb, rather than leave him completely helpless, placed Rankin's revolver back into its holster. He didn't care to think what it would be like to regain consciousness only to face, weaponless, a predator drawn by the scent of blood, and by the sight of a man too hurt to defend himself.

Convinced he'd done all he could, Burn Wheelock mounted again and gave his animal the spur. He glanced back once, at Sam Rankin sitting propped against a tree and the black horse tied nearby; then they dropped from sight behind him, and he was alone.

* * *

Now that he could set his own pace, the distance remaining shouldn't take much time. He bore in mind that the old wagon horse was going to have to do further duty, helping haul the rig up to get the sheriff—there was the dun, of course, but he wasn't sure Homer Flagg's horse would work in harness; still, from necessity he gave the animal considerable of a workout. By the time they came at last into the ranchyard, his mount had worked up a sweat and its sides were beginning to work like bellows.

Not to waste time, he went directly to the barn where he left the animal standing, not bothering yet to strip the gear. Inside, the wagon harness was hung neatly on the rack he had built for it. He was just reaching to take it down when, behind him in the quiet of the barn, he heard the voice that chilled his blood.

'Don't bother with the harness,' Homer Flagg said. 'Just keep your hands high, and

233

face me.'

Numb with shock, Wheelock made himself do as he was told; he came slowly around, and saw the shape of the man leaning against a roof prop, and the metallic gleam of gun-metal held casually in one big hand. Wheelock tried to speak, found his voice on the second attempt. 'What—what are you doing here?'

'Waitin' for you,' the other said pleasantly. He pushed erect and prowled forward, the gun an unspoken threat. He flipped aside the front of Wheelock's jacket, making sure the prisoner wore no weapon.

'We brung some beef for our old friend Telford,' he explained. 'Never knew he was dead, till we learned it from his women. Didn't know about *you* being here; then I seen my old dun horse out in the corral. We just moved the beef out of sight into the timber—didn't want you seein' anything to scare you off. We've took turns watching.'

Now, as his eyes adjusted, Wheelock could see there were horses in all the barn's four stalls, standing under saddles; one, he thought, looked like his own blue roan. Four of the Flaggs were here, then—maybe more, if they had horses hidden other places besides the barn...

One frightening question was beating around in his brain, clamoring for an answer. 'What have you done to—?'

'The women? They're at the house,' Homer

234

said pleasantly. 'With Pa and the others. Just go on over.'

He stood there grinning, glints of red shining in unshaven whiskers. He must have known Burn Wheelock couldn't put up any resistance; he wasn't even bothering any longer to threaten him with the gun. Wheelock's shoulders sagged. Without another word he turned, and walked out of the barn. He drew a breath into cramped lungs, and started directly across the yard toward the house.

The door was shut, the windows like blank and unseeing eyes that told him nothing of what might be happening there. But now, behind him, big Homer let out a piercing blast on two fingers. The whistle was a signal; next moment the door swung open and Noah's gray-maned bulk filled the opening. He looked out at Wheelock, and he lifted an arm and motioned him in. There was a kind of wolfish intensity about him as he stood waiting.

Wheelock knew he had no option, no way to refuse. Stolidly he moved on across the sunlit yard, and up to the door; Noah pushed the screen open for him and Burn Wheelock walked in, to deliver himself into the hands of his enemies.

CHAPTER SEVENTEEN

They had been forcing the women to cook for them.

Wheelock saw that the table held the wreckage of a gargantuan meal. A couple of the Flaggs—Mason, and another he thought answered to the name of Quincy—were busily shoveling away ham and biscuits and greens and stewed tomatoes; as he entered, Susan was serving up a fresh platter of fried eggs and browned potatoes, with Mase just about to help himself to a generous portion. Everybody froze, gone motionless as they stared at Wheelock in the doorway.

He looked past them, quickly hunting for Rebecca. She stood by the stove, an iron coffeepot in her hand. She looked pale, and dazed with shock. But when he asked her bluntly, 'Have they hurt you any?' the girl shook her head and silently mouthed her answer, *No.*

Thank God for that, he thought fervently. And then Noah grabbed him by a shoulder, and he looked up into a hatred that made the ugly wall eyes gleam with fury. Noah said thickly, 'So at last I got my hands on you! The sonofabitch that murdered my boy Chet!'

A sour freight of whiskey smell rode his breath—Wheelock had seen the half-empty bottles on the table, and now he realized that all these men were reeling drunk, dangerous and beyond reason. Still, he had to try to talk sense to them.

'I never murdered anybody. There was three of them against me, and I was fighting for my life!'

'And my boy Rufe,' the old man went on doggedly, as though he hadn't heard. His big hands twitched with the desire to punish.

Burn Wheelock would not give up trying. 'What happened to Rufe was none of my doing. I swear!'

'Hell! It was done with your rope...'

'I'm sick and tired of hearing about that rope! Jess Croy took it away from me and hanged him with it. When I tried to interfere, Croy used his gun barrel on me.' He added, 'And today I killed him!'

That caused a stir. Noah's mismatched eyes were working furiously, studying his face. 'You killed Jess Croy?' Suspicion edged the old man's voice. 'If so, where's his carcass?'

'Why—' Suddenly his voice failed him. For he was thinking of Sam Rankin, lying wounded up there where Wheelock had left him. Even if he led these men by some other route to show them Croy's body, they'd be bound to see the sign of a third horseman. They'd never be satisfied until they checked it out; and all at once it chilled his blood, to think what could happen if these men were to find

237

their enemy—the tough Wasco County sheriff—helpless and hurt and completely at their mercy. No question about it; they'd seize the chance to finish him off!

They read their own meaning, now, into Burn Wheelock's hesitation. Mase said heavily, 'Hell! He's lying. And even if he did kill Croy for us—he'd still have Chet to answer for!'

'But I—'

It was as far as he got. Noah Flagg swore at him and suddenly those work-gnarled hands, like small shovels, were swinging and he was being struck open-palmed, left and right, his head rocking on his shoulders as he stumbled back under the onslaught. He brought up against the wall, hard, and the blows held him pinned there. His hat fell to the floor. Buzzing darkness began to fill his skull and he felt warm blood gush from his nose.

Just as abruptly, the beating stopped. By stiffening his wobbly knees and pressing his shoulders against the wall he was just able to stay upright; and now, through the ringing in his head as it began slowly to clear, he was aware of Rebecca's sobbing voice. He focused his eyes, with an effort. The girl was struggling in the hands of Quincy Flagg, using the most surprising and unladylike language as she fought to get free and come to Burn Wheelock's aid.

Noah said impatiently, 'Damn it, boy! Keep

238

her quiet!'

Quincy began shaking her, violently, so that her head wobbled and her hair came down from its pins. Wheelock cried out but was still far too dazed to make any move toward helping her. When at last Quincy let her go, subdued and with the breath shaken out of her, Susan was there to take her daughter into her arms. Noah grunted, in satisfaction, 'That's better!' And turned his attention again to Burn Wheelock.

Somehow, the latter found his voice. 'Don't hurt the women!' he cried, past the tang of blood in his mouth. He could no longer hope to do anything for himself, or for Sam Rankin who was going to have to survive somehow on his own; but there was one thing he might still accomplish and he put into it all the desperate earnestness and persuasion he had left. 'Whatever you intend doing to me, just don't do it in front of *them*! Go away and leave them in peace, and I won't give you any trouble. I promise!'

In the doorway, Homer Flagg said, 'Look who thinks he's in a position to bargain!'

Wheelock hadn't seen the big fellow come in, following him from the barn. Homer eyed the prisoner's bloody face and demanded of his father, in some irritation, 'Why are we takin' so much time? Hell, he knows what's gonna happen to him; let's get on with it. I've had this ready for somebody, ever since Rufe got his.'

239

And he showed them his hands. One held a coil of yellow rope; something rose in Burn Wheelock's throat as he saw, dangling from the other, the loop and the thirteen wraps of an expertly fashioned hangman's knot. 'Some good-sized pine at the foot of the meadow, there below the barn,' Homer continued, with the assurance of one who had already scouted them with a particular need in mind. 'Just right to do this job...'

A sound of horror broke from Rebecca. She was staring at the rope, her face gone completely colorless; Wheelock thought she would make some foolish move but her mother's arm about her shoulders prevented her. Oddly enough, it was Susan who found the temerity to face these creatures and exclaim, 'What in the world kind of men *are* you? How can you stand here and talk about something like—like—?' She couldn't say the word.

Noah looked at her in real, if boozy, surprise. Plainly he had not expected any such outburst from this timid little woman; but then, neither had Burn Wheelock. The old man reminded her, 'My son Rufe was a man, and they done it to *him*.'

'Rufe Flagg was a cattle thief!' Wheelock cried, unable to keep it back. 'Like all his kin!'

With a roar, old Noah turned and struck him full across the mouth, bringing blood as his lip split against a tooth. And then, pointing a finger at Homer, he shouted, 'Go on—fetch the sonofabitch a horse. We'll take care of him, right now!'

At that, Homer showed all his teeth in an eager grin. He spied one of the whiskey bottles on the table and paused long enough to grab it up; afterward, slamming out through the door, he was off across the yard at a run, the coiled rope swinging. He left a buzz of drunken excitement behind him—and no question in Wheelock's numbed mind as to what was about to happen to him.

Of all these men, only Mason—the clever one—seemed sober enough to have any doubts about what they were doing. He said now, 'What do we do with the women?'

'Bring 'em along,' Noah grunted. 'Do 'em good, to learn we mean business.'

'But that makes them witnesses,' Mase objected. 'What they ain't seen with their own eyes, they can't talk about later.'

'Hell!' The look Noah gave the two of them was enough to curdle the blood. 'If they ain't fools, they'll know better than to talk. They won't say one damn word...'

'For God's sake!' Burn Wheelock reached and caught frantically at Noah's arm. 'Please! *Don't make them watch this!*'

Slowly, Noah turned his head. He looked at the hand that clutched his sleeve, and then those terrible mismatched eyes lifted to Wheelock's face. What he might have read there—what unfamiliar stirring of compassion

241

might have been raised in him—it would have been impossible to say. But, however grudgingly, he shrugged and threw a look at Mason. 'You want to stay here, then—and keep an eye on them?'

'And miss the show?' Mase retorted. 'Hell, no! Quincy can stay.'

'Me?' Quincy was primed at once to argue, but apparently the pecking order in the Flagg family held firm and they paid him not the slightest heed. As he stood there, grumbling and mean-tempered and ignored, Noah turned on the prisoner. He caught Wheelock by a shoulder, whirled him and thrust him toward the door. The screen slammed wide. With Rebecca's cry of protest sounding in his head, Wheelock stumbled out into the sunlight.

He was given no chance to catch his footing. A hand in the middle of his back shoved him forward, so that he missed the next step and went spilling to the ground on his face. He landed painfully; dazed and bloody, it took him a moment to find strength to push himself up and get his knees under him. As he did so, he was aware of shod hoofs shaking the earth. He lifted his head, and there was Homer Flagg spurring toward him, brandishing rope and whiskey bottle. He was riding the blue roan.

For all his own predicament, Burn Wheelock could feel a surge of hot anger as he saw the new, red spur marks that scored its flanks. These few days in Homer's possession had been cruel ones for Wheelock's pony. He tried to swear at the man but there was dust in his throat and no sound came out, that he could hear. Homer Flagg had pulled rein directly in front of him, yanking the roan's head back hard. While the animal danced nervously under this treatment, Homer tilted the whiskey bottle to his mouth, drained off the last of its contents, flung it away in a smear of sun on splintering glass.

And then he was shaking out his rope, and with a quick dabbing motion dropped its loop over the head of the man who knelt before him.

Wheelock guessed what was coming and made a supreme effort to scramble to his feet. But a jerk of the rope threw him off again, twirled him and dropped him onto his back; sky and clouds and ranch buildings wheeled around him. He had just a glimpse of the door and of Rebecca, with pure horror in her face, trying to fight her way to him. She was seized and hauled back, and Quincy's solid frame showed briefly before the door slammed shut.

Homer kicked with the spurs. Burn Wheelock caught frantically at the rope as the roan leaped forward and he was hauled twisting and turning in the wake of the galloping animal, like a fish played on a line. Dust filled his eyes and gaping mouth; the noose at his throat cut off his wind; panic filled him at the imminent likelihood of being dragged to death.

This could have lasted no more than seconds, before movement stopped and through the pound of blood in his ears he heard Mason Flagg yelling angrily at his brother: 'Damn it, you're gonna have the job done before we even find a tree!'

'Let him keep up, then!'

Wheelock felt himself raised and set on his feet, by a lift of the rope. This time when the roan went into motion he was able, dazed as he was, to keep his boots under him, in a staggering run. He stumbled briefly and thought his head would be yanked from his shoulders; but somehow he managed to keep going with Noah and Mase flanking him on either side, laughing and shouting drunkenly— across the barren yard and then, with grass and weeds catching at his boots and trying to trip him up, down the slope of the meadow beyond.

Tree shadows closed over him. The rope slammed him hard against a pine and Burn Wheelock slid down the trunk, rough bark catching at his clothing. But now, suddenly, there was stillness. He pawed frantically at the noose that seemed imbedded in his throat; he got his fingers under it, worked it loose enough for cool, welcome air to pour into his lungs.

He was given only a moment's respite. After that hands were on him, roughly hauling him to his feet. He felt himself being lifted, felt the hard saddle under him and his boots being guided into the stirrups—and, like Rufe Flagg

244

on that other day, he all at once found the strength of terror and began to fight. He lashed out, heard cursing voices, felt hands on his clothing and shook them off, put a boot into someone's chest. A heavy fist struck him above the ear and all but knocked the wits out of him. It was all futile, of course, but he couldn't die without a struggle...

Homer, between yells at the others to control their prisoner, had been trying to toss an end of his rope across a high limb and cursing every time he missed. Suddenly he vented an exclamation of triumph. He promptly flung his whole weight upon the rope and the noose at once clenched tight, the knot pressing hard behind Wheelock's ear. For a sickening instant the prisoner's boots rode free of their stirrups. Blood roared through his head; he felt his eyes starting from their sockets, his tongue swelling to fill his mouth. Dimly, he heard Homer shouting orders: 'That's got him! Now, damn it, tie his hands! Use a belt if you got nothing else...'

Wheelock's arms were jerked behind him; smooth leather touched his wrists and began to bind them. Daylight was fading and strengthening again, with every throb of the pain behind his eyeballs...

It was in this pulsation of splintered light and dark that he saw an apparition take shape before him. It looked almost like a horse with a man on its back, a man who carried one shoulder grotesquely higher than the other and his head dropped forward upon his chest. The first clear hint that this strange figure was real, and not something out of Wheelock's tortured head, came when the hands that grappled with him suddenly fell away and the man spoke—incredibly, with the voice of Sam Rankin: 'Thought you could lose me a second time, Wheelock? Thought I was too far gone to make it into the saddle? Damn you, when will you learn—?'

The voice broke off suddenly, with an oath. And then: *'Flagg!'*

Burn Wheelock, all at once realizing his hands were free and that the rope had gone slack, groped to paw at it and jerk it loose—and, this time, fling it over his head and away from him in convulsive horror. He was sobbing for air as he twisted about on the saddle, trying to learn what was happening. There was Homer, standing by the roan's head and glaring at the sheriff. And Wheelock saw the gun rising in Homer's big fist.

He couldn't take time to think; he simply dropped from the saddle, on top of the man. It was like tackling a tree. Yet, for all his size, Homer couldn't stand against the dead weight that landed on his shoulders, bearing him down. Wheelock had managed to hook an arm about his throat, and force his head back; they landed solidly with the big man underneath. Homer bucked and struggled to dislodge his

246

opponent. He spewed curses and whiskey fumes into Wheelock's face. But somehow the smaller man was able to keep his throat lock, and with what strength he had left he put on the pressure.

Somewhere very near, a gunshot sounded, then two more.

The frightened roan tried to wheel and an iron hoof struck Wheelock's shin and seemed almost to break it. He shouted with the pain of it; Homer Flagg managed to shake off his hold, at the same time sinking an elbow into his middle and driving most of the wind from him. Through a haze of pain Wheelock saw the man's right fist come up. It still held the revolver—desperately he reached and tried to trap it. Homer Flagg rolled from under him, breaking away.

When the gun went off, without warning, the report was muffled.

Burn Wheelock got shakily to his feet.

He didn't want to see what the bullet had done—the sudden jerk and as sudden limpness of Homer's body told him enough. He looked around, stunned and struck by the quiet. He saw the blue roan had escaped, but Sam Rankin's rented livery horse still stood. Its saddle was empty.

Burn Wheelock searched hastily, thoroughly expecting to see the sheriff lying on the ground, lifeless. But it was Noah Flagg who sprawled with blood on his chest, the lank gray hair fanned out around his dead face and unseeing eyes. Sam Rankin was on his knees, doubled forward, one hand propping him up; the other held a gun. He peered up through a balloon of powder smoke at Mason Flagg, who stood motionless with hands half raised, apparently not quite ready to brave the sheriff's weapon.

Knees still unsteady, Burn Wheelock got to Mase and lifted the revolver out of his holster; and as though that released him from the supreme effort he was making, Sam Rankin dropped his weapon and simply folded and pitched quietly forward on his face in the litter of pine needles.

Looking at Mason, Wheelock tried to speak, had to clear his tortured throat a time or two before words would come out. 'Your pa and your brother are both dead. Do *you* want to try something!' But Mason, who had always shown more brains than the rest of them, read his look and seemed disinclined. He stood stiffly motionless while the other went to Rankin's body, and leaned for the handcuffs in the lawman's pocket. At sight of them Mason's eyes shone hotly but he offered no resistance. He let himself be turned about and shoved up against a pine tree, and made to embrace the trunk with his arms; when the cuffs clicked into place Burn Wheelock said tersely, 'That takes care of *you* for a while!'

He turned anxiously to the sheriff.

248

It had been simply weakness, and not another bullet, that knocked Rankin from his saddle. Wheelock got him propped up and carefully inspected the bandaging, but could find no fresh bleeding. 'I'm through worrying about you,' he said gruffly. 'Nobody's going to kill you—you're too damn mean!'

Wheelock wasn't absolutely sure the sheriff heard him. Rankin's face was drained of its usual color, its lean and raw-boned lines appeared to sag. But Wheelock saw the tawny eyes focused on him and he knew then the officer was listening. He told the man, 'I want you to get this straight: I didn't run out on you today! I had to leave you while I come down to fetch a wagon—only, when I got here I run into a nest of rattlers.

'You know what I found out? Them Flaggs told me Reub Telford was one of their fences! There ought to be some beef here in the timber right now that will help to prove it!'

Rankin seemed to consider that, his pain-wracked face dark with thought. 'I ain't too surprised,' he admitted finally. 'It fits what I'd heard of Telford.'

Wheelock drew a breath. 'I got one more piece of news,' he said. 'And that is—I ain't going back with you. That's final! I been hounded from all sides, for something that wasn't my doing to start with, and I've had enough! I don't aim to stand for any more.'

The other's stare burned into his own; then,

249

as with an effort, Sam Rankin tipped his head forward in a nod. 'All right, Wheelock. Have it your way! Write me out a deposition: the whole story—the Flaggs, and killing Jess Croy—all of it. I guess I can make do with that.'

Even wounded and helpless as he was, Burn Wheelock understood that in wringing that concession out of the sheriff he finally had won a battle of wills. But he didn't let on that he knew this. All he said was, 'Sure.'

Rankin wasn't quite finished. 'I might have to call on you—just as a favor, you know'—and a hint of humor tilted the corners of the bitter mouth—'in case I bring what's left of the Flaggs to trial and need a witness. But we got the worst ones. Maybe the threat will be enough to hold the rest of them in line.' His glance drifted meaningfully to Mason Flagg, who stood with shackled arms wrapped around the trunk of a pine tree, and Noah and Homer dead on the ground beside him. Yes, Burn Wheelock thought, the sheriff was right. They'd got the worst ones...

But that reminded him, and brought him surging to his feet exclaiming, 'Oh, my God—I forgot! The women! They're at the house, alone with one of them—'

At that moment, almost as if in answer to his thought, he heard someone hurrying toward him through the trees. When Rebecca's voice called his name, tremulous with anxiety, Wheelock broke into a run himself. He saw

250

her, then—her fair hair in a tangle, her eyes a stain in her white face, both hands encumbered by the awkward weight of a long-barreled revolver. With a cry she flung herself at Wheelock, so desperately that he was staggered; he dropped his own gun and caught her close.

She looked up at his bloody face, and at the marks where the rope had torn his throat; a moan of sympathy broke from her as she reached up to touch him. 'Oh, Burn! Oh, *darling*!'

It seemed suddenly a very natural thing for her to call him; he hardly even stopped to marvel at it. Instead, pointing at the revolver he demanded hoarsely, 'Where did you get that?'

She looked at it a moment as though she couldn't remember. 'I was coming to try and *help*,' she said finally. 'That man they left with us—the one they called Quincy? When we heard the shooting he seemed to forget all about Mama and me. He went to the window for a look—and she had the frying pan handy...'

Wheelock stared. 'Your mother hit Quincy Flagg with a fry pan?'

'Just as hard as she could!' Rebecca answered, and giggled a little. Next moment the giggles turned to hysterical sobs and she was in his arms again, pressed tight, her tear-wet face against his shirt.

His tough, hard hand caressed her shoulder. 'Now, Becky,' he said gently. 'Becky...' And though it was the first time, it seemed a very natural thing, too, for him to call her that.

D(wight) B(ennett) Newton is the author of a number of notable Western novels. Born in Kansas City, Missouri, Newton went on to complete work for a Master's degree in history at the University of Missouri. From the time he first discovered Max Brand in Street and Smith's WESTERN STORY MAGAZINE, he knew he wanted to be an author of Western fiction. He began contributing Western stories and novelettes to the Red Circle group of Western pulp magazines published by Newsstand in the late 1930s. During the Second World War, Newton served in the U.S. Army Engineers and fell in love with the central Oregon region when stationed there. He would later become a permanent resident of that state and Oregon frequently serves as the locale for many of his finest novels. As a client of the August Lenniger Literary Agency, Newton found that every time he switched publishers he was given a different byline by his agent. This complicated his visibility. Yet in notable novels from RANGE BOSS (1949), the first original novel ever published in a modern paperback edition, through his impressive list of titles for the Double D series from Doubleday, THE OREGON RIFLES, CROOKED RIVER CANYON, and DISASTER CREEK among them, he produced a very special kind of Western story. What makes it so special is the combination of characters who seem real and about whom a

253

reader comes to care a great deal and Newton's fundamental humanity, his realization early on (perhaps because of his study of history) that little that happened in the West was ever simple but rather made desperately complicated through the conjunction of numerous opposed forces working at cross purposes. Yet, through all of the turmoil on the frontier, a basic human decency did emerge. It was this which made the American frontier experience so profoundly unique and which produced many of the remarkable human beings to be found in the world of Newton's Western fiction.

We hope you have enjoyed this Large Print book. Other Chivers Press or G.K. Hall & Co. Large Print books are available at your library or directly from the publishers.

For more information about current and forthcoming titles, please call or write, without obligation, to:

Chivers Press Limited
Windsor Bridge Road
Bath BA2 3AX
England
Tel. (01225) 335336

OR

G.K. Hall & Co.
P.O. Box 159
Thorndike, Maine 04986
USA
Tel. (800) 223–2336

All our Large Print titles are designed for easy reading, and all our books are made to last.